BIG SUR

First Warbler Classics Edition 2019

First published by Farrar, Straus & Cudahy in 1962

www.warblerpress.com

ISBN 978-1-7340292-6-0 (paperback)
ISBN 978-1-7340292-7-7 (e-book)

BIG SUR

Jack Kerouac

Author's Note

My work comprises one vast book like Proust's except that my remembrances are written on the run instead of afterwards in a sick bed. Because of the objections of my early publishers I was not allowed to use the same personae names in each work. On the Road, The Subterraneans, The Dharma Bums, Doctor Sax, Maggie Cassidy, Tristessa, Desolation Angels, Visions of Cody *and the others including this book* Big Sur *are just chapters in the whole work which I call* The Duluoz Legend. *In my old age I intend to collect all my work and re-insert my pantheon of uniform names, leave the long shelf full of books there, and die happy. The whole thing forms one enormous comedy, seen through the eyes of poor Ti Jean (me), otherwise known as Jack Duluoz, the world of raging action and folly and also of gentle sweetness seen through the keyhole of his eye.*

JACK KEROUAC

Contents

1

THE CHURCH IS BLOWING a sad windblown "Kathleen" on the bells in the skid row slums as I wake up all woebegone and goopy, groaning from another drinking bout and groaning most of all because I'd ruined my "secret return" to San Francisco by getting silly drunk while hiding in the alleys with bums and then marching forth into North Beach to see everybody altho Lorenz Monsanto and I'd exchanged huge letters outlining how I would sneak in quietly, call him on the phone using a code name like Adam Yulch or Lalagy Pulvertaft (also writers) and then he would secretly drive me to his cabin in the Big Sur woods where I would be alone and undisturbed for six weeks just chopping wood, drawing water, writing, sleeping, hiking, etc. etc.— But instead I've bounced drunk into his City Lights bookshop at the height of Saturday night business, everyone recognized me (even tho I was wearing my disguise-like fisherman's hat and fishermen coat and pants waterproof) and 't'all ends up a roaring drunk in all the famous bars the bloody "King of the Beatniks" is back in town buying drinks for everyone—Two days of that, including Sunday the day Lorenzo is supposed to pick me up at my "secret" skid row hotel (the Mars on 4th and Howard) but when he calls for me there's no answer, he has the clerk open the door and what does he see but me out on the floor among bottles, Ben Fagan stretched out partly beneath the bed, and Robert Browning the beatnik painter out on the bed, snoring—So says to himself "I'll pick him up next weekend, I guess he wants to drink for a week in the city (like he always does, I guess)" so off he drives to his Big Sur cabin without me thinking he's doing the right thing but my God when I wake up, and Ben and Browning are gone, they've somehow dumped me on the bed, and I hear "I'll Take You Home Again Kathleen" being bellroped so sad in the fog winds out there that blow across the rooftops of eerie old hangover Frisco, wow, I've hit the end of the trail and cant even drag my body any more even

to a refuge in the woods let alone stay upright in the city a minute—
It's the first trip I've taken away from home (my mother's house) since
the publication of "Road" the book that "made me famous" and in fact
so much so I've been driven mad for three years by endless telegrams,
phonecalls, requests, mail, visitors, reporters, snoopers (a big voice
saying in my basement window as I prepare to write a story:—ARE
YOU BUSY?) or the time the reporter ran upstairs to my bedroom as
I sat there in my pajamas trying to write down a dream—Teenagers
jumping the six-foot fence I'd had built around my yard for privacy—
Parties with bottles yelling at my study window "Come on out and
get drunk, all work and no play makes Jack a dull boy!"—A woman
coming to my door and saying "I'm not going to ask you if you're
Jack Duluoz because I know he wears a beard, can you tell me where
I can find him, I want a real beatnik at my annual Shindig party"—
Drunken visitors puking in my study, stealing books and even pencils—Uninvited acquaintances staying for days because of the clean
beds and good food my mother provided—Me drunk practically all
the time to put on a jovial cap to keep up with all this but finally
realizing I was surrounded and outnumbered and had to get away to
solitude again or die—So Lorenzo Monsanto wrote and said "Come
to my cabin, no one'll know," etc. so I had sneaked into San Francisco
as I say, coming 3000 miles from my home in Long Island (Northport)
in a pleasant roomette on the California Zephyr train watching
America roll by outside my private picture window, really happy for
the first time in three years, staying in the roomette all three days and
three nights with my instant coffee and sandwiches—Up the Hudson
Valley and over across New York State to Chicago and then the Plains,
the mountains, the desert, the final mountains of California, all so
easy and dreamlike compared to my old harsh hitch hikings before I
made enough money to take transcontinental trains (all over America
highschool and college kids thinking "Jack Duluoz is 26 years old
and on the road all the time hitch hiking" while there I am almost
40 years old, bored and jaded in a roomette bunk crashin across that
Salt Flat)—But in any case a wonderful start towards my retreat so
generously offered by sweet old Monsanto and instead of going thru
smooth and easy I wake up drunk, sick, disgusted, frightened, in fact

terrified by that sad song across the roofs mingling with the lachry-
mose cries of a Salvation Army meeting on the corner below "*Satan* is
the cause of your alcoholism, *Satan* is the cause of your immorality,
Satan is *everywhere* workin to destroy you unless you repent *now*" and
worse than that the sound of old drunks throwing up in rooms next
to mine, the creak of hall steps, the moans everywhere—Including the
moan that had awakened me, my own moan in the lumpy bed, a moan
caused by a big roaring Whoo Whoo in my head that had shot me out
of my pillow like a ghost.

2

AND I LOOK AROUND THE DISMAL CELL, there's my hopeful rucksack all neatly packed with everything necessary to live in the woods, even unto the minutest first aid kit and diet details and even a neat little sewing kit cleverly reinforced by my good mother (like extra safety pins, buttons, special sewing needles, little aluminum scissors)—The hopeful medal of St. Christopher even which she'd sewn on the flap—The survival kit all in there down to the last little survival sweater and handkerchief and tennis sneakers (for hiking)—But the rucksack sits hopefully in a strewn mess of bottles all empty, empty poorboys of white port, butts, junk, horror. . . . "One fast move or I'm gone," I realize, gone the way of the last three years of drunken hopelessness which is a physical and spiritual and metaphysical hopelessness you cant learn in school no matter how many books on existentialism or pessimism you read, or how many jugs of vision-producing Ayahuasca you drink, or Mescaline take, or Peyote goop up with—That feeling when you wake up with the delirium tremens with the *fear* of eerie death dripping from your ears like those special heavy cobwebs spiders weave in the hot countries, the feeling of being a bentback mudman monster groaning underground in hot steaming mud pulling a long hot burden nowhere, the feeling of standing ankledeep in hot boiled pork blood, ugh, of being up to your waist in a giant pan of greasy brown dishwater not a trace of suds left in it—The face of yourself you see in the mirror with its expression of unbearable anguish so hagged and awful with sorrow you cant even cry for a thing so ugly, so lost, no connection whatever with early perfection and therefore nothing to connect with tears or anything: it's like William Seward Burroughs' "Stranger" suddenly appearing in your place in the mirror—Enough! "One fast move or I'm gone" so I jump up, do my headstand first to pump blood back into the hairy brain, take a shower in the hall, new T-shirt and socks and underwear, pack vigorously, hoist the rucksack and run out throwing the key on the desk and hit the cold street and walk fast to the nearest little grocery store to buy two days of food, stick it in the rucksack, hike thru lost alleys of Russian sorrow where bums sit head on knees in foggy doorways in the goopy eerie city night I've got to escape or die, and into the bus station—In a half hour into a bus seat, the bus says "Monterey" and off we go down the clean neon hiway and I sleep all the way, waking up amazed and well again smelling sea air the bus driver shaking me "End of the line, Monterey."—And by God it *is* Monterey, I stand sleepy in the 2 A.M. seeing vague little fishing masts across the street from the bus drive-way. Now all I've got to do to complete my escape is get 14 miles down the coast to the Raton Canyon bridge and hike in.

3

"ONE FAST MOVE OR I'M GONE" so I blow $8 on a cab to drive me down that coast, it's a foggy night tho sometimes you can see stars in the sky to the right where the sea is, tho you cant see the sea you can only hear about it from the cabdriver—"What kinda country is it around here? I've never seen it."

"Well, you cant see it tonight—Raton Canyon you say, you better be careful walkin around there in the dark."

"Why?"

"Well, just use your lamp like you say—"

And sure enough when he lets me off at the Raton Canyon bridge and counts the money I sense something wrong somehow, there's an awful roar of surf but it isnt coming from the right place, like you'd expect it to come from "over there" but it's coming from "under there"—I can see the bridge but I can see nothing below it—The bridge continues the coast highway from one bluff to another, it's a nice white bridge with white rails and there's a white line runnin down the middle familiar and highwaylike but something's wrong—Besides the headlights of the cab just shoot out over a few bushes into empty space in the direction where the canyon's supposed to be, it feels like being up in the air somewhere tho I can see the dirt road at our feet and the dirt overhang on the side—"What in the hell is this?"—I've got the directions all memorized from a little map Monsanto's mailed me but in my imagination dreaming about this big retreat back home there'd been something larkish, bucolic, all homely woods and gladness instead of all this aerial roaring mystery in the dark—When the cab leaves I therefore turn on my railroad lantern for a timid peek but its beam gets lost just like the car lights in a void and in fact the battery is fairly weak and I can hardly see the bluff at my left—As for the bridge I cant see it anymore except for graduating series of luminous shoulder buttons going off further into the low sea roar—The sea roar is bad enough except it keeps bashing and barking at me like a dog in the fog down there, sometimes it booms the earth but my God where is the earth and how can the sea be underground!—"The only thing to do," I gulp, "is to put this lantern shinin right in front of your feet, *kiddo*, and follow that lantern and make sure it's shinin on the road rut and hope and pray it's shinin on ground that's gonna be there when it's shining," in other words I actually fear that even my lamp will carry me astray if I dare to raise it for a minute from the ruts in the dirt road—The only satisfaction I can glean from this roaring high horror of darkness is that the lamp wobbles huge dark shadows of its little rim stays on the overhanging bluff at the left of the road, because to the right (where the bushes are wiggling in the wind from the sea) there aint no shadows because there aint no light can take hold—So I start my trudge, pack aback, just head down following my lamp spot, head down but eyes suspiciously peering a little up, like a man in the presence of a dangerous idiot he doesnt want to annoy— The dirt road starts up a little, curves to the right, starts down a little, then suddenly up again, and up—By now the sea roar is further back and at one point I even stop and look back to see nothing—"I'm gonna put out my light and see what I can see" I say rooted to my feet where they're rooted to that road—Fat lotta good, when I put out the light I see nothing but the dim sand at my feet.

Trudging up and getting further away from the sea roar I get to feel more confident but suddenly I come to a frightening thing in the road, I stop and hold out my hand, edge forward, it's only a cattle crossing (iron bars imbedded across the road) but at the same time a big blast of wind comes from the left where the bluff should be and I spot that way and see nothing. "What the hell's going on!" "Follow the road," says the other voice trying to be calm so I do but the next instant I hear a rattling to my right, throw my light there, see nothing but bushes wiggling dry and mean and just the proper high canyonwall kind of bushes fit for rattlesnakes too—(which it was, a rattlesnake doesnt like to be awakened in the middle of the night by a trudging humpbacked monster with a lamp.)

But now the road's going down again, the reassuring bluff reappears on my left, and pretty soon according to my memory of Lorry's map there she is, the creek, I can hear her lappling and gabbing down there at the bottom of the dark where at least I'll be on level ground and done with booming airs somewhere above—But the closer I get to the creek as the road dips steeply, suddenly, almost making me trot forward, the louder it roars, I begin to think I'll fall right into it before I can notice it—It's screaming like a raging flooded river right below me—Besides it's even *darker* down there than anywhere! There are glades down there, ferns of horror and slippery logs, mosses, dangerous plashings, humid mists rise coldly like the breath of death, big dangerous trees are beginning to bend over my head and brush my pack—There's a noise I know can only grow louder as I sink down and for fear how loud it can grow I stop and listen, it rises up crashing mysteriously at me from a raging battle among dark things, wood or rock or something cracked, all smashed, all wet black sunken earth danger—I'm *afraid* to go down there—I am *affrayed* in the old Edmund Spenser sense of being *frayed* by a whip, and a wet one at that—A slimy green dragon racket in the bush—An angry war that doesnt want me pokin around—It's been there a million years and it doesnt want me clashing darkness with it—It comes snarling from a thousand crevasses and monster redwood roots all over the map of creation—It is a dark clangoror in the rain forest and doesnt want no skid row bum to carry to the sea which is bad enough and waitin back there—I can almost feel the sea pulling at that racket in the trees but there's my spotlamp so all I gotta do is follow the lovely sand road which dips and dips in rising carnage and suddenly a flattening, a sight of bridge logs, there's the bridge rail, there's the creek just four feet below, cross the bridge you woken bum and see what's on the other shore.

Take one quick peek at the water as you cross, just water over rocks, a small creek at that.

And now before me is a dreamy meadowland with a good old corral gate and a barbed wire fence the road running right on left but this where I get off at last. Then I crawl thru the barbed wire and find myself trudging a sweet little sand road winding right thru fragrant dry heathers as tho I'd just popped thru from hell into familiar old Heaven on Earth, yair and Thank God (tho a minute later my heart's in my mouth again because I see black things in the white sand ahead but it's only piles of good old mule dung in Heaven).

4

AND IN THE MORNING (after sleeping by the creek in the white sand) I do see what was so scary about my canyon road walk—The road's up there on the wall a thousand feet with a sheer drop sometimes, especially at the cattle crossing, way up highest, where a break in the bluff shows fog pouring through from another bend of the sea beyond, scary enough in itself anyway as tho one hole wasnt enough to open into the sea—And worst of all is the bridge! I go ambling seaward along the path by the creek and see this awful thin white line of bridge a thousand unbridgeable sighs of height above the little woods I'm walking in, you just cant believe it, and to make things heart-thumpingly horrible you come to a little bend in what is now just a trail and there's the booming surf coming at you whitecapped crashing down on sand as tho it was higher than where you stand, like a sudden tidal wave world enough to make you step back or run back to the hills—And not only that, the blue sea behind the crashing high waves is full of huge black rocks rising like old ogresome castles dripping wet slime, a billion years of woe right there, the moogrus big clunk of it right there with its slaverous lips of foam at the base—So that you emerge from pleasant little wood paths with a stem of grass in your teeth and drop it to see doom—And you look up at that unbelievably high bridge and feel death and for a good reason: because underneath the bridge, in the sand right beside the sea cliff, *hump,* your heart sinks to see it: the automobile that crashed thru the bridge rail a decade ago and fell 1000 feet straight down and landed upsidedown, is still there now, an upsidedown chassis of rust in a strewn skitter of sea-eaten tires, old spokes, old car seats sprung with straw, one sad fuel pump and no more people—

Big elbows of Rock rising everywhere, sea caves within them, seas plollocking all around inside them crashing out foams, the boom and pound on the sand, the sand dipping quick (no Malibu Beach

here)—Yet you turn and see the pleasant woods winding upcreek like
a picture in Vermont—But you look up into the sky, bend way back,
my God you're standing directly under that aerial bridge with its thin
white line running from rock to rock and witless cars racing across it
like dreams! From rock to rock! All the way down the raging coast!
So that when later I heard people say "Oh Big Sur must be beautiful!"
I gulp to wonder why it has the reputation of being beautiful above
and beyond its *fearfulness*, its Blakean groaning roughrock Creation
throes, those vistas when you drive the coast highway on a sunny day
opening up the eye for miles of horrible washing sawing.

5

IT WAS EVEN FRIGHTENING at the other peaceful end of Raton Canyon,
the east end, where Alf the pet mule of local settlers slept at night such
sleepfull sleeps under a few weird trees and then got up in the morning to graze in the grass then negotiated the whole distance slowly to
the sea shore where you saw him standing by the waves like an ancient
sacred myth character motionless in the sand—Alf the Sacred Burro
I later called him—The thing that was frightening was the mountain that rose up at the east end, a strange Burmese like mountain
with levels and moody terraces and a strange ricepaddy hat on top
that I kept staring at with a sinking heart even at first when I was
healthy and feeling good (and I would be going mad in this canyon
in six weeks on the fullmoon night of September 3rd)—The mountain reminded me of my recent recurrent nightmares in New York
about the "Mountain of Mien Mo" with the swarms of moony flying
horses lyrically sweeping capes over their shoulders as they circled the
peak a "thousand miles high" (in the dream it said) and on top of the
mountain in one haunted nightmare I'd seen the giant empty stone
benches so silent in the topworld moonlight as tho once inhabited by
Gods or giants of some kind but long ago vacated so that they were
all dusty and cobwebby now and the evil lurked somewhere inside
the pyramid nearby where there was a monster with a big thumping heart but also, even more sinister, just ordinary seedy but muddy
janitors cooking over small woodfires—Narrow dusty holes through
which I'd tried to crawl with a bunch of tomato plants tied around
my neck—Dreams—Drinking nightmares—A recurrent series of
them all swirling around that mountain, seen the very first time as
a beautiful but somehow horribly green verdant mist enshrouded
jungle peak rising out of green tropical country in "Mexico" so called
but beyond which were pyramids, dry rivers, other countries full
of infantry enemy and yet the biggest danger being just hoodlums

out throwing rocks on Sundays—So that the sight of that simple sad
mountain, together with the bridge and that car that had flipped over
twice or so and landed flump in the sand with no more sign of human
elbows or shred neckties (like a terrifying poem about America you
could write), agh, HOO HOO of Owls living in old evil hollow trees
in that misty tangled further part of the canyon where I was always
afraid to go anyhow—That unclimbably tangled steep cliff at the base
of Mien Mo rising to gawky dead trees among bushes so dense and
up to heathers God knows how deep with hidden caves no one not
even I spose the Indians of the 10th Century had ever explored—And
those big gooky rainforest ferns among lightningstruck conifers right
beside sudden black vine cliff faces rising right at your side as you
walk the peaceful path—And as I say that ocean coming at you higher
than you are like the harbors of old woodcuts always higher than the
towns (as Rimbaud pointed out shuddering)—So many evil combi-
nations even unto the bat who would come at me later while I slept
on the outdoor cot on the porch of Lorenzo's cabin, come circle my
head coming real low sometimes filling me with the traditional fear
it'll get tangled in my hair, and such silent wings, how would you like
to wake up in the middle of the night and see silent wings beating
over you and you ask yourself "Do I really believe in Vampires?"—In
fact, flying silently around my lamplit cabin at 3 o'clock in the morning as I'm reading (of all things) (shudder) *Doctor Jekyll and Mister
Hyde*—Small wonder maybe that I myself turned from serene Jekyll to
hysterical Hyde in the short space of six weeks, losing absolute control
of the peace mechanisms of my mind for the first time in my life.

But Ah, at first there were fine days and nights, right after Monsanto
drove me to Monterey and back with two boxes of a full grub list and
left me there alone for three weeks of solitude, as we'd agreed—So
fearless and happy I even spotted his powerful flashlight up at the
bridge the first night, right thru the fog the eerie finger reaching the
pale bottom of that high monstrosity, and even spotted it out over the
farmless sea as I sat by caves in the crashing dark in my fisherman's
outfit writing down what the sea was saying—Worst of all spotting
it up at those tangled mad cliffsides where owls hooted ooraloo—
Becoming acquainted and swallowing fears and settling down to life

in the little cabin with its warm glow of woodstove and kerosene lamp
and let the ghosts fly their asses off—The Bhikku's home in his woods,
he only wants peace, peace he will get—Tho why after three weeks
of perfect happy peace and adjustment in these strange woods my
soul so went down the drain when I came back with Dave Wain and
Romana and my girl Billie and her kid, I'll never know—Worth the
telling only if I dig deep into everything.

Because it was so beautiful at first, even the circumstance of my
sleepingbag suddenly erupting feathers in the middle of the night as
I turned over to sleep on, so I curse and have to get up and sew it by
lamplight or in the morning it might be empty of feathers—And as I
bend poor mother head over my needle and thread in the cabin, by
the fresh fire and in the light of the kerosene lamp, here come those
damned silent black wings flapping and throwing shadows all over my
little home, the bloody bat's come in my house—Trying to sew a poor
patch on my old crumbly sleepingbag (mostly ruined by my having to
sweat out a fever inside of it in a hotel room in Mexico City in 1957
right after the gigantic earthquake there), the nylon all rotten almost
from all that old sweat, but still soft, tho so soft I have to cut out a piece
of old shirt flap and patch over the rip—I remember looking up from
my middle of the night chore and saying bleakly "They, yes, have bats
in Mien Mo valley"—But the fire crackles, the patch gets sewn, the
creek gurgles and thumps outside—A creek having so many voices
it's amazing, from the kettledrum basin deep bumpbumps to the little
gurgly feminine crickles over shallow rocks, sudden choruses of other
singers and voices from the log dam, dibble dabble all night long and
all day long the voices of the creek amusing me so much at first but in
the later horror of that madness night becoming the babble and rave
of evil angels in my head—So not minding the bat or the rip finally,
ending up cant sleep because too awake now and it's 3 A.M. so the
fire I stoke and I settle down and read the entire *Doctor Jekyll and
Mister Hyde* novel in the wonderful little handsized leather book left
there by smart Monsanto who also must've read it with wide eyes on
a night like that—Ending the last elegant sentences at dawn, time to
get up and fetch water from gurgly creek and start breakfast of pan-
cakes and syrup—And saying to myself "So why fret when something

goes wrong like your sleepingbag breaking in the night, use self reliance"—"Screw the bats" I add.

Marvelous opening moment in fact of the first afternoon I'm left alone in the cabin and I make my first meal, wash my first dishes, nap, and wake up to hear the rapturous ring of silence or Heaven even within and throughout the gurgle of the creek—When you say AM ALONE and the cabin is suddenly home only because you made one meal and washed your firstmeal dishes—Then nightfall, the religious vestal fighting of the beautiful kerosene lamp after careful washing of the mantle in the creek and careful drying with toilet paper, which spoils it by specking it so you again wash it in the creek and this time just let the mantle drip dry in the sun, the late afternoon sun that disappears so quickly behind those giant high steep canyon walls—Nightfall, the kerosene lamp casts a glow in the cabin, I go out and pick some ferns like the ferns of the Lankavatara Scripture, those hairnet ferns, "Look sirs, a beautiful hairnet!"—Late afternoon fog pours in over the canyon walls, sweep, cover the sun, it gets cold, even the flies on the porch are as so sad as the fog on the peaks—As daylight retreats the flies retreat like polite Emily Dickinson flies and when it's dark they're all asleep in trees or someplace—At high noon they're in the cabin with you but edging further towards the open doorsill as the afternoon lengthens, how strangely gracious—There's the hum of the bee drone two blocks away the racket of it you'd think it was right over the roof, when the bee drone swirls nearer and nearer (gulp again) you retreat into the cabin and wait, maybe they got a message to come and see you all two thousand of em—But getting used to the bee drone finally which seems to happen like a big party once a week—And so everything eventually marvelous.

Even the first frightening night on the beach in the fog with my notebook and pencil, sitting there crosslegged in the sand facing all the Pacific fury flashing on rocks that rise like gloomy sea shroud towers out of the cove, the bingbang cove with its seas booming inside caves and slapping out, the cities of seaweed floating up and down you can even see their dark leer in the phosphorescent seabeach nightlight—That first night I sit there and all I know, as I look up, is the kitchen light is on, on the cliff, to the right, where somebody's just built a cabin overlooking all the horrible Sur, somebody up there's having a mild and tender supper that's all I know—The lights from the cabin kitchen up there go out like a little weak lighthouse beacon and ends suspended a thousand feet over the crashing shore—Who would build a cabin up there but some bored but hoary old adventurous architect maybe got sick of running for congress and one of these days a big Orson Welles tragedy with screaming ghosts a woman in a white nightgown'll go flying down that sheer cliff—But actually in my mind what I really see is the kitchen lights of that mild and tender maybe even romantic supper up there, in all that howling fog, and here I am way below in the Vulcan's Forge itself looking up with sad eyes—Blanking my little Camel cigarette on a billion year old rock that rises behind my head to a height unbelievable—The little kitchen light on the cliff is only on the end of it, behind it the shoulders of the great sea hound cliff go rising up and back and sweeping inland higher and higher till I gasp to think "Looks like a reclining dog, big friggin shoulders on that sonofabitch"—Riseth and sweepeth and scareth men to death but what is death anyway in all this water and rock.

I fix up my sleepingbag on the porch of the cabin but at 2 A.M. the fog starts dripping all wet so I have to go indoors with wet sleepingbag and make new arrangements but who cant sleep like a log in a solitary cabin in the woods, you wake up in the late morning so refreshed and realizing the universe namelessly: the universe is an Angel—But easy enough to say when you've had your escape from the gooky city turn into a success—And it's finally only in the woods you get that nostalgia for "cities" at last, you dream of long gray journeys to cities where soft evenings'll unfold like Paris but never seeing how sickening it will be because of the primordial innocence of health and stillness in the wilds—So I tell myself "Be Wise."

6

THOUGH THERE ARE FAULTS to Monsanto's cabin like no screened windows to keep the flies out in the daytime just big board windows, so that also on foggy days when it's damp if you leave them open it's too cold, if you leave them closed you cant see anything and have to light the lamp at noon—And but for that no other faults—It's all marvelous—And at first it's so amazing to be able to enjoy dreamy afternoon meadows of heather up the other end of the canyon and just by walking less than a halfmile you can suddenly also enjoy wild gloomy sea coast, or if you're sick of either of these just sit by the creek in a gladey spot and dream over snags—So easy in the woods to daydream and pray to the local spirits and say "Allow me to stay here, I only want peace" and those foggy peaks answer back mutely Yes—And to say to yourself (if you're like me with theological preoccupations) (at least at that time, before I went mad I still had such preoccupations) "God who is everything possesses the eye of awakening, like dreaming a long dream of an impossible task and you wake up in a flash, oops, No Task, it's done and gone"—And in the flush of the first few days of joy I confidently tell myself (not expecting what I'll do in three weeks only) "no more dissipation, it's time for me to quietly watch the world and even enjoy it, first in woods like these, then just calmly walk and talk among people of the world, no booze, no drugs, no binges, no bouts with beatniks and drunks and junkies and everybody, no more I ask myself the question *O why is God torturing me,* that's it, be a loner, travel, talk to waiters only, in fact, in Milan, Paris, just talk to waiters, walk around, no more self imposed agony . . . it's time to think and watch and keep concentrated on the fact that after all this whole surface of the world as we know it now will be covered with the silt of a billion years in time . . . Yay, for this, more aloneness"—"Go back to childhood, just eat apples and read your Cathechism—sit on curbstones, the hell with the hot lights of Hollywood" (remembering

that awful time only a year earlier when I had to rehearse my reading
of prose a third time under the hot lights of the Steve Allen Show in
the Burbank studio, one hundred technicians waiting for me to start
reading, Steve Allen watching me expectant as he plunks the piano,
I sit there on the dunce's stool and refuse to read a word or open my
mouth, "I dont have to REHEARSE for God's sake Steve!"—"But go
ahead, we just wanta get the tone of your voice, just this last time, I'll
let you off the dress rehearsal" and I sit there sweating not saying a
word for a whole minute as everybody watches, finally I say "No I cant
do it" and I go across the street to get drunk) (but surprising everybody the night of the show by doing my job of reading just fine, which
surprises the producers and so they take me out with a Hollywood
starlet who turns out to be a big bore trying to read me her poetry
and wont talk love because in Hollywood man love is for sale)—So
even that marvelous, long remembrances of life all the time in the
world to just sit there or lie there or walk about slowly remembering
all the details of life which now because a million lightyears away have
taken on the aspect (as they must've for Proust in his sealed room)
of pleasant mental movies brought up at will and projected for further study—And pleasure—As I imagine God to be doing this very
minute, watching his own movie, which is us.

Even when one night I'm so happy sighin to turn over to resume
my sleep but a rat suddenly runs over my head, it's marvelous because
I then take the folding cot and put a big wide board on it that covers
both sides, so I wont sink into the canvas confines there, and place
two old sleepingbags over the board, then my own on top, I have the
most marvelous and rat free and in fact healthy-for-the-back bed in
the world.

I also take long curious hikes to see what's what in the other direction inland, going up a few miles along the dirt road that leads to
isolated ranches and logging camps—I come to giant sad quiet val-
leys where you see 150 foot tall redwood trees with sometimes one
little bird right on the topmost peaktwig sticking straight up—The
bird balances up there surveying the fog and the great trees—You see
one single flower nodding on a cliff side far across the canyon, or a
huge knot in a redwood tree looking like Zeus' face, or some of God's

little crazy creations goofing around in creek pools (zigzag bugs), or a sign on a lonely fence saying "M.P.Passey, No Trespassing," or terraces of fern in the dripping redwood shade, and you think "A long way from the beat generation, in this rain forest"—So I angle back down to the home canyon and down the path past the cabin and out to the sea where the mule is on the sea shore, nibbling under that one thousand foot bridge or sometimes just standing staring at me with big brown Garden of Eden eyes—The mule being a pet of one of the families who have a cabin in the canyon and it, as I say Alf by name, just wanders from one end of the canyon where the corral fence stops him, to the wild seashore where the sea stops him but a strange Gauguinesque mule when you first see him, leaving his black dung on the perfect white sand, an immortal and primordial mule owning a whole valley—I even finally later find out where Alf sleeps which is like a sacred grove of trees in that dreaming meadow of heather—So I feed Alf the last of my apples which he receives with big faroff teeth inside his soft hairy muzzle, never biting, just muffing up my apple from my outstretched palm, and chomping away sadly, turning to scratch his behind against a tree with a big erotic motion that gets worse and worse till finally he's standing there with erectile dong that would scare the Whore of Babylon let alone me.

All kinds of strange and marvelous things like the weird Ripley situation of a huge tree that's fallen across a creek maybe 500 years ago and's made a bridge thereby, the other end of its trunk is now buried in ten feet of silt and foliage, strange enough but out of the middle trunk over the water rises straight another redwood tree looking like it's been plated in the treetrunk, or stuck down into it by a God hand, I cant figure it out and stare at this chewing furiously on big choking handfulls of peanuts like a college boy—(and only weeks before falling on my head in the Bowery)—Even when a rancher car goes by I day-dream mad ideas like, here comes Farmer Jones and his two daughters and here I am with a 60-foot redwood tree under my arm walking slowly pulling it along, they are amazed and scared, "Are we dreaming? can anybody be that strong?" they even ask me and my big Zen answer is "You only think I'm strong" and I go on down the road carrying my tree—This has me laughing in clover fields for hours—I pass a cow which turns to look at me as it takes a big dreamy crap—Back in the cabin I light the fire and sit sighing and there are leaves skittering on the tin roof, it's August in Big Sur—I fall asleep in the chair and when I wake up I'm facing the thick little tangled woods outside the door and I suddenly remember them from long ago, even to the particular clumpness of the thickets, stem by stem, the twist of them, like an old home place, but just as I'm wondering what all this mess is, bang, the wind closes the cabin door on my sight of it!—So I conclude "I see as much as doors'll allow, open or shut"—Adding, as I get up, in a loud English Lord voice nobody can hear anyway, "An issue broached is an issue smote, Sire," pronouncing "issue" like "iss-yew"—And this has me laughing all through supper—Which is pota-toes wrapped in foil and thrown on the fire, and coffee, and hunks of Spam roasted on a spit, and applesauce and cheese—And when I light the lamp of aftersupper reading, here comes the nightly moth to his nightly death at my lamp—After I put out the lamp temporarily, there's the moth sleeping on the wall not realizing I've put it on again.

Meanwhile by the way and however, every day is cold and cloudy, or damp, not cold in the eastern sense, and every night is absolutely fog: no stars whatever to be seen—But this too turns out to be a marvelous circumstance as I find out later, it's the "damp season" and the other dwellers (weekenders) of the canyon dont come out on weekends, I'm absolutely alone for weeks on end (because later in August when the sun conquered the fog suddenly I was amazed to hear laughing and scratching all up and down the valley which had been mine only mine, and when I tried to go to the beach to squat and write there were whole families having outings, some of them younger people who'd simply parked their cars up on the high bridge bluff and climbed down) (some of them in fact gangs of yelling hoodlums)—So the rain-forest summer fog was grand and besides when the sun prevailed in August a horrible development took place, huge blasts of frightening gale like wind came pouring into the canyon making all the trees roar with a really frightening intensity that sometimes built up to a boom-ing war of trees that shook the cabin and woke you up—And was in fact one of the things that contributed to my mad fit.

But the most marvelous day of all when I completely forgot who I was where I was or the time a day just with my pants rolled up above my knees wading in the creek rearranging the rocks and some of the snags so that the water where I stooped (near the sandy shore) to get jugfuls would, instead of just sluggishly passing by shallow over mud, with bugs in it, now come rushing in a pure gurgly clear stream and deep too—I dug into the white sand and arranged underground rocks so now I could stick a jug in there and tilt the opening to the stream and it would fill up instantly with clear rushing unstagnated bugless drinking water—Making a mill race, is what it's called—And because now the water rushed so fast and deep right by the sandy stooping place I had to build a kind of seawall of rocks against that rush so that the shore would not be silted away by the race—Doing that, fortifying the outside of the seawall with smaller rocks and finally at sundown with bent head over my sniffling endeavors (the way a kid sniffles when he's been playing all day) I start inserting tiny pebbles in the spaces between the stones so that no water can sneak over to wash away the shore, even down to the tiniest sand, a perfect sea wall, which I top with a wood plank for everybody to kneel on when they come there to fetch their holy water—Looking up from this work of an entire day, from noon till sundown, amazed to see where I was, who I was, what I'd done—The absolute innocence like of Indian fashioning a canoe all alone in the woods—And as I say only weeks earlier I'd fallen flat on my head in the Bowery and everybody thought I'd hurt myself—So I make supper with a happy song and go out in the foggy moonlight (the moon sent its white luminescence through) and marveled to watch the new swift gurgling clear water run with its pretty flashes of light—"And when the fog's over and the stars and the moon come out at night it'll be a beautiful sight."

And such things—A whole mess of little joys like that amazing me when I came back in the horror of later to see how they'd all changed and become sinister, even my poor little wood platform and mill race when my eyes and my stomach nauseous and my soul screaming a thousand babbling words, oh—It's hard to explain and best thing to do is not be false.

7

BECAUSE ON THE FOURTH day I began to get bored and noted it in my diary with amazement, "Already bored?"—Even tho the handsome words of Emerson would shake me out of that where he says (in one of those little redleather books, in the essay on "Self Reliance" a man "is relieved and gay when he has put his heart into his work and done his best") (applicable both to building simple silly little millraces and writing big stupid stories like this)—Words from that trumpet of the morning in America, Emerson, he who announced Whitman and also said "Infancy conforms to nobody"—The infancy of the simplicity of just being happy in the woods, conforming to nobody's idea about what to do, what should be done—"Life is not an apology"—And when a vain and malicious philanthropic abolitionist accused him of being blind to the issues of slavery he said "Thy love afar is spite at home" (maybe the philanthropist had Negro help anyway)—So once I again I'm Ti Jean the Child, playing, sewing patches, cooking suppers, washing dishes (always kept the kettle boiling on the fire and anytime dishes need to be washed I just pour hot hot water into pan with Tide soap and soak them good and then wipe them clean after scouring with little 5-&-10 wire scourer)—Long nights simply thinking about the usefulness of that little wire scourer, those little yellow copper things you buy in supermarkets for 10 cents, all to me infinitely more interesting than the stupid and senseless "Steppenwolf" novel in the shack which I read with a shrug, this old fart reflecting the "conformity" of today and all the while he thought he was a big Nietzsche, old imitator of Dostoevsky 50 years too late (he feels tormented in a "personal hell" he calls it because he doesnt like what other people like!)—Better at noon to watch the orange and black Princeton colors on the wings of a butterfly—Best to go hear the sound of the sea at night on the shore.

Maybe I shouldna gone out and scared or bored or belabored

myself so much, tho, on that beach at night which would scare any
ordinary mortal—Every night around eight after supper I'd put on my
big fisherman coat and take the notebook, pencil and lamp and start
down the trail (sometimes passing ghostly Alf on the way) and go
under that frightful high bridge and see through the dark fog ahead
the white mouths of ocean coming high at me—But knowing the ter-
rain I'd walk right on, jump the beach creek, and go to my corner
by the cliff not far from one of the caves and sit there like an idiot in
the dark writing down the sound of the waves in the notebook page
(secretarial notebook) which I could see white in the darkness and
therefore without benefit of lamp scrawl on—I was afraid to light my
lamp for fear I'd scare the people way up there on the cliff eating their
nightly tender supper—(later found out there was nobody up there
eating tender suppers, they were overtime carpenters finishing the
place in bright lights)—And I'd get scared of the rising tide with its 15
foot waves yet sit there hoping in faith that Hawaii warnt sending no
tidal wave I might miss seeing in the dark coming from miles away
high as Groomus—One night I got scared anyway so sat on top of 10
foot cliff at the foot of the big cliff and the waves are going "Rare, he
rammed the gate rare"—"Raw roo roar"—"Crowsh"—the way waves
sound especially at night—The sea not speaking in sentences so much
as in short lines: "Which one? . . . the one ploshed?. . . . the same, ah
Boom" . . . Writing down these fantastic inanities actually but yet I felt
I had to do it because James Joyce wasnt about to do it now he was dead
(and figuring "Next year I'll write the different sound of the Atlantic
crashing say on the night shores of Cornwall, or the soft sound of the
Indian Ocean crashing at the mouth of the Ganges maybe")—And I
just sit there listening to the waves talk all up and down the sand in
different tones of voice "Ka bloom, kerplosh, ah ropey otter barnacled
be, crowsh, are rope the angels in all the sea?" and such—Looking up
occasionally to see rare cars crossing the high bridge and wondering
what they'd see on this drear foggy night if they knew a madman was
down there a thousand feet below in all that windy fury sitting in
the dark writing in the dark—Some sort of sea beatnik, tho anybody
wants to call me a beatnik for THIS better try it if they dare—The
huge black rocks seem to move—The bleak awful roaring isolateness,

no ordinary man could do it I'm telling you—*I am a Breton!* I cry and
the blackness speaks back "*Les poissons de la mer parlent Breton*" (the
fishes of the sea speak Breton)—Nevertheless I go there every night
even tho I dont feel like it, it's my duty (and probably drove me mad),
and write these sea sounds, and all the whole insane poem "Sea."

Always so wonderful in fact to get away from that and back to
the more human woods and come to the cabin where the fire's still
red and you can see the Bodhisattva's lamp, the glass of ferns on the
table, the box of Jasmine tea nearby, all so gentle and human after that
rocky deluge out there—So I make an excellent pan of muffins and tell
myself "Blessed is the man can make his own bread"—Like that, the
whole three weeks, happiness—And I'm rolling my own cigarettes,
too—And as I say sometimes I meditate how wonderful the fantastic
use I've gotten out of cheap little articles like the scourer, but in this
instance I think of the marvelous belongings in my rucksack like my
25 cent plastic shaker with which I've just made the muffin batter but
also I've used it in the past to drink hot tea, wine, coffee, whisky and
even stored clean handkerchiefs in it when I traveled—The top part
of the shaker, my holy cup, and had it for five years now—And other
belongings so valuable compared to the worthlessness of expensive
things I'd bought and never used—Like my black soft sleeping sweater
also five years which I was now wearing in the damp Sur summer
night and day, over a flannel shirt in the cold, and just the sweater
for the night's sleep in the bag—Endless use and virtue of it!—And
because the expensive things were of ill use, like the fancy pants
I'd bought for recent recording dates in New York and other tele-
vision appearances and never even wore again, useless things like a
$40 raincoat I never wore because it didnt even have slits in the side
pockets (you pay for the label and the so called "tailoring")—Also an
expensive tweed jacket bought for TV and never worn again—Two
silly sports shirts bought for Hollywood never worn again and were
9 bucks each!—And it's almost tearful to realize and remember the
old green T-shirt I'd found, mind you, eight years ago, mind you, on
the DUMP in Watsonville California mind you, and got fantastic use
and comfort from it—Like working to fix that new stream in the creek
to flow through the convenient deep new waterhole near the wood

platform on the bank, and losing myself in this like a kid playing, it's the little things that count (clichés are truisms and all truisms are true)—On my deathbed I could be remembering that creek day and forgetting the day MGM bought my book, I could be remembering the old lost green dump T-shirt and forgetting the sapphired robes— Mebbe the best way to get into Heaven.

I go back to the beach in the daytime to write my "Sea," I stand there barefoot by the sea stopping to scratch one ankle with one toe, I hear the rhythm of those waves, and they're saying suddenly "Is Virgin you trying to fathom me"—I go back to make a pot of tea.

> Summer afternoon—
> Impatiently chewing
> The Jasmine leaf

At high noon the sun always coming out at last, strong, beating down on my nice high porch where I sit with books and coffee and the noon I thought about the ancient Indians who must have inhabited this canyon for thousands of years, how even as far back at the 10th Century this valley must have looked the same, just different trees: these ancient Indians simply the ancestors of the Indians of only recently say 1860—How they've all died and quietly buried their grievances and excitements—How the creek may have been an inch deeper since logging operations of the last 60 years have removed some of the watershed in the hills back there—How the women pounded the local acorns, acorns or shmacorns, I finally found the natural nuts of the valley and they were sweet tasting—And men hunted deer—In fact God knows what they did because I wasnt here—But the same valley, a thousand years of dust more or less over their footsteps of 960 A.D.—And as far as I can see the world is too old for us to talk about it with our new words—We will pass just as quietly through life (passing through, passing through) as the 10th century people of this valley only with a little more noise and a few bridges and dams and bombs that wont even last a million years—The world being just what it is, moving and passing through, actually alright in the long view and nothing to complain about—Even the rocks of the valley had

earlier rock ancestors, a billion billion years ago, have left no howl of
complaint—Neither the bee, or the first sea urchins, or the clam, or
the severed paw—All sad So-Is sight of the world, right there in front
of my nose as I look,—And looking at that valley in fact I also realize
I have to make lunch and it wont be any different than the lunch of
those olden men and besides it'll taste good—Everything is the same,
the fog says "We are fog and we fly by dissolving like ephemera," and
the leaves say "We are leaves and we jiggle in the wind, that's all, we
come and go, grow and fall"—Even the paper bags in my garbage pit
say "We are man-transformed paper bags made out of wood pulp, we
are kinda proud of being paper bags as long as that will be possible, but
we'll be mush again with our sisters the leaves come rainy season"—
The tree stumps say "We are tree stumps torn out of the ground by
men, sometimes by wind, we have big tendrils full of earth that drink
out of the earth"—Men say "We are men, we pull out tree stumps, we
make paper bags, we think wise thoughts, we make lunch, we look
around, we make a great effort to realize everything is the same"—
While the sand says "We are sand, we already know," and the sea says
"We are always come and go, fall and plosh"—The empty blue sky of
space says "All this comes back to me, then goes again, and comes back
again, then goes again, and I dont care, it still belongs to me"—The
blue sky adds "Dont call me eternity, call me God if you like, all of you
talkers are in paradise: the leaf is paradise, the tree stump is paradise,
the paper bag is paradise, the man is paradise, the sand is paradise,
the sea is paradise, the man is paradise, the fog is paradise"—Can you
imagine a man with marvelous insights like these can go mad within
a month? (because you must admit all those talking paper bags and
sands were telling the truth)—But I remember seeing a mess of leaves
suddenly go skittering in the wind and into the creek, then floating
rapidly down the creek towards the sea, making me feel a nameless
horror even then of "Oh my God, we're all being swept away to sea no
matter what we know or say or do"—And a bird who was on a crooked
branch is suddenly gone without my even hearing him.

8

BUT THERE'S MOONLIT FOGNIGHT, the blossoms of the fire flames in
the stove—There's giving an apple to the mule, the big lips taking
hold—There's the bluejay drinking my canned milk by throwing his
head back with a miffle of milk on his beak—There's the scratching
of the raccoon or of the rat out there, at night—There's the poor little
mouse eating her nightly supper in the humble corner where I've put
out a little delight-plate full of cheese and chocolate candy (for my
days of killing mice are over)—There's the raccoon in his fog, there
the man to his fireside, and both are lonesome for God—There's me
coming back from seaside nightsittings like a muttering old Bhikku
stumbling down the path—There's me throwing my spotlight on a
sudden raccoon who clambers up a tree his little heart beating with
fear but I yell in French "Hello there little man" (*allo ti bonhomme*)—
There's the bottle of olives, 49¢, imported, pimentos, I eat them one
by one wondering about the late afternoon hillsides of Greece—And
there's my spaghetti with tomato sauce and my oil and vinegar salad
and my applesauce *relishe* my dear and my black coffee and Roquefort
cheese and afterdinner nuts, my dear, all in the woods—(Ten delicate
olives slowly chewed at midnight is something no one's ever done in
luxurious restaurants)—There's the present moment fraught with tangled woods—There's the bird suddenly quiet on his branch while his
wife glances at him—There's the grace of an axe handle as good as an
Eglevsky ballet—There's "Mien Mo Mountain" in the fog illumined
August moon mist among other heights gorgeous and misty rising in
dimmer tiers somehow rosy in the night like the classic silk paintings
of China and Japan—There's a bug, a helpless little wingless crawler,
drowning in a water can, I get it out and it wanders and goofs on the
porch till I get sick of watching—There's the spider in the outhouse
minding his own business—There's my side of bacon hanging from a
hook on the ceiling of the shack—There's the laughter of the loon in the

shadow of the moon—There's an owl hooting in weird Bodhidharma trees—There's flowers and redwood logs—There's the simple woodfire and the careful yet absentminded feeding of it which is an activity that like all activities is no-activity (*Wu Wei*) yet it is a meditation in itself especially because all woodfires, like snowflakes, are different every time—Yes, there's the resinous purge of a flame-enveloped redwood log—Yes the cross-sawed redwood log turns into a coal and looks like a City of the Gandharvas or like a western butte at sunset—There's the bhikku's broom, the kettle—There's the laced soft fud over the sand, the sea—There's all these avid preparations for decent sleep like the night I'm looking for my sleeping socks (so's not to dirty the sleeping-bag inside) and find myself singing "A donde es me sockiboos?"—Yes, and down in the valley there's my burro, Alf, the only living being in sight—There's in mid of sleep the moon appearing—There's universal substance which is divine substance because where else can it be?—There's the family of deer on the dirt road at dusk—There's the creek coughing down the glade—There's the fly on my thumb rubbing its nose then stepping to the page of my book—There's the hummingbird swinging his head from side to side like a hoodlum—There's all that, and all my fine thoughts, even unto my ditty written to the sea "I took a pee, into the sea, acid to acid, and me to ye" yet I went crazy inside three weeks.

For who could go crazy that could be so relaxed as that: but wait: there are the signposts of something wrong.

9

THE FIRST SIGNPOST CAME AFTER that marvelous day I went hiking up
the canyon road again to the highway at the bridge where there was a
rancher mailbox where I could dump mail (a letter to my mother and
saying in it give a kiss to Tyke, my cat, and a letter to old buddy Julien
addressed to Coaly Rustnut from Runty Onenut) and as I walked way
up there I could see the peaceful roof of my cabin way below and half
mile away in the old trees, could see the porch, the cot where I slept,
and my red handkerchief on the bench beside the cot (a simple little
sight: of my handkerchief a half mile away making me unaccountably
happy)—And on the way back pausing to meditate in the grove of trees
where Alf the Sacred Burro slept and seeing the roses of the unborn in
my closed eyelids just as clearly as I had seen the red handkerchief and
also my own footsteps in the seaside sand from way up on the bridge,
saw, or heard, the words "Roses of the Unborn" as I sat crosslegged in
soft meadow sand, heard that awful stillness at the heart of life, but
felt strangely low, as tho premonition of the next day—When I went to
the sea in the afternoon and suddenly took a huge deep Yogic breath
to get all that good sea air in me but somehow just got an overdose of
iodine, or of evil, maybe the sea caves, maybe the seaweed cities, something, my heart suddenly beating—Thinking I'm gonna get the local
vibrations instead here I am almost fainting only it isnt an ecstatic
swoon by St. Francis, it comes over me in the form of horror of an
eternal condition of sick mortality in me—In me and in everyone—I
felt completely nude of all poor protective devices like thoughts about
life or meditations under trees and the "ultimate" and all that shit,
in fact the other pitiful devices of making supper or saying "What I
do now next? chop wood?"—I see myself as just doomed, pitiful—An
awful realization that I have been fooling myself all my life thinking
there was a next thing to do to keep the show going and actually I'm
just a sick clown and so is everybody else—All all of it, pitiful as it

is, not even really any kind of commonsense animate effort to ease the soul in this horrible sinister condition (of mortal hopelessness) so I'm left sitting there in the sand after having almost fainted and stare at the waves which suddenly are not waves at all, with I guess what must have been the goopiest downtrodden expression God if He exists must've ever seen in His movie career—*Éh vache*, I hate to write—All my tricks laid bare, even the realization that they're laid bare itself laid bare as a lotta bunk—The sea seems to yell to me GO TO YOUR DESIRE DONT HANG AROUND HERE—For after all the sea must be like God, God isnt asking us to mope and suffer and sit by the sea in the cold at midnight for the sake of writing down useless sounds, he gave us the tools of self reliance after all to make it straight thru bad life mortality towards Paradise maybe I hope—But some miserables like me dont even know it, when it comes to us we're amazed—Ah, life is a gate, a way, a path to Paradise anyway, why not live for fun and joy and love or some sort of girl by a fireside, why not go to your desire and LAUGH . . . but I ran away from that seashore and never came back again without that secret knowledge: that it didnt want me there, that I was a fool to sit there in the first place, the sea has its waves, the man has his fireside, period.

That being the first indication of my later flip—But also on the day of leaving the cabin to hitch hike back to Frisco and see everybody and by now I'm tired of my food (forgot to bring jello, you need jello after all that bacon fat and cornmeal in the woods, every woodsman needs jello) (or cokes) (or something)—But it's time to leave, I'm now so scared by that iodine blast by the sea and by the boredom of the cabin I take 20 dollars worth of perishable food left and spread it out on a big board below the cabin porch for the bluejays and the raccoon and the mouse and the whole lot, pack up, and go—But before I go I realize this isnt my own cabin (here's the second signpost of my madness), I have no right to hide Monsanto's rat poison, as I've been doing, feeding the mouse instead, as I said—So like a dutiful guest in another man's cabin I take the cover off the rat poison but compromise by simply leaving the box on the top shelf, so nobody can complain—And go off like that—But during my absence, but—You'll see.

10

WITH MY MIND EVEN AND UPRIGHT and abiding nowhere, as Hui Neng would say, I go dancing off like a fool from my sweet retreat, rucksack on back, after only three weeks and really after only 3 or 4 days of boredom, and go hankering back for the city—"You go out in joy and in sadness you return," says Thomas à Kempis talking about all the fools who go forth for pleasure like high school boys on Saturday night hurrying clacking down the sidewalk to the car adjusting their ties and rubbing their hands with anticipatory zeal, only to end up Sunday morning groaning in bleary beds that Mother has to make anyway—It's a beautiful day as I come out of that ghostly canyon road and step out on the coast highway, just this side of Raton Canyon bridge, and there they are, thousands and thousands of tourists driving by slowly on the high curves all oo ing and aa ing at all that vast blue panorama of seas washing and raiding at the coast of California—I figure I'll get a ride into Monterey real easy and take the bus there and be in Frisco by nightfall for a big ball of wino yelling with the gang, I feel in fact Dave Wain oughta be back by now, or Cody will be ready for a ball, and there'll be girls, and such and such, forgetting entirely that only three weeks previous I'd been sent fleeing from that gooky city by the horrors—But hadnt the sea told me to flee back to my own reality?

But it is beautiful especially to see up ahead north a vast expanse of curving seacoast with inland mountains dreaming under slow clouds, like a scene of ancient Spain, or properly really like a scene of the real essentially Spanish California, the old Monterey pirate coast right there, you can see what the Spaniards must've thought when they came around the bend in their magnificent sloopies and saw all that dreaming fatland beyond the seashore whitecap doormat—Like the land of gold—The old Monterey and Big Sur and Santa Cruz magic— So I confidently adjust my pack straps and start trudging down the road looking back over my shoulder to thumb.

This is the first time I've hitch hiked in years and I soon begin to see that things have changed in America, you cant get a ride any more (but of course especially on a strictly tourist road like this coast highway with no trucks or business)—Sleek long stationwagon after wagon comes sleering by smoothly, all colors of the rainbow and pastel at that, pink, blue, white, the husband is in the driver's seat with a long ridiculous vacationist hat with a long baseball visor making him look witless and idiot—Beside him sits wifey, the boss of America, wearing dark glasses and sneering, even if he wanted to pick me up or anybody up she wouldn't let him—But in the two deep backseats are children, children, millions of children, all ages, they're fighting and screaming over ice cream, they're spilling vanilla all over the Tartan seatcovers— There's no room anymore anyway for a hitch hiker, tho conceivably the poor bastard might be allowed to ride like a meek gunman or silent murderer in the very back platform of the wagon, but here no, alas! here is ten thousand racks of drycleaned and perfectly pressed suits and dresses of all sizes for the family to look like millionaires every time they stop at a roadside dive for bacon and eggs—Every time the old man's trousers start to get creased a little in the front he's made to take down a fresh pair of slacks from the back rack and go on, like that, bleakly, tho he might have secretly wished just a good oldtime fishing trip alone or with his buddies for this year's vacation—But the P.T.A. has prevailed over every one of his desires by now, 1960's, it's no time for him to yearn for Big Two Hearted River and the old sloppy pants and the string of fish in the tent, or the woodfire with Bourbon at night—It's time for motels, roadside driveins, bringing napkins to the gang in the car, having the car washed before the return trip—And if he thinks he wants to explore any of the silent secret roads of America it's no go, the lady in the sneering dark glasses has now become the navigator and sits there sneering over her previously printed blue-lined roadmap distributed by happy executives in neckties to the vacationists of America who would also wear neckties (after having come along so far) but the vacation fashion is sports shirts, long visored hats, dark glasses, pressed slacks and baby's first shoes dipped in gold oil dangling from the dashboard—So here I am standing in that road with that big woeful rucksack but also probably with that expression of horror on my face after all those nights sitting in the seashore under giant black cliffs, they see in me the very apotheosical opposite of their every vacation dream and of course drive on—That afternoon I say about 5 thousand cars or probably 3 thousand passed me not one of them ever dreamed of stopping—Which didnt bother me anyway because at first seeing that gorgeous long coast up to Monterey I thought "Well I'll just hike right in, it's only 14 miles, I oughta do that easy"—And on the way there's all kindsa interesting things to see anyway like the seals barking on rocks below, or quiet old farms made of logs on the hills across the highway, or sudden upstretches that go along dreamy seaside meadows where cows grace and graze in full sight of endless blue Pacific—But because I'm wearing desert boots with their fairly thin soles, and the sun is beating hot on the tar road, the heat finally gets through the soles and I begin to deliver heat blisters in my sockiboos—I'm limping along wondering what's the matter with me when I realize I've got blisters—I sit by the side of the road and look—I take out my first aid kit from the pack and apply unguents and put on cornpads and carry on—But the combination of the heavy pack and the heat of the road increases the pain of the blisters until finally I realize I've got to hitch hike a ride or never make it to Monterey at all.

But the tourists bless their hearts after all, they couldnt know, only think I'm having a big happy hike with my rucksack and they drive on, even tho I stick out my thumb—I'm in despair because I'm really stranded now, and by the time I've walked seven miles I still have seven to go but I cant go on another step—I'm also thirsty and there are absolutely no filling stations or anything along the way—My feet are ruined and burned, it develops now into a day of complete torture, from nine o'clock in the morning till four in the afternoon I negotiate those nine or so miles when I finally have to stop and sit down and wipe the blood off my feet—And then when I fix the feet and put the shoes on again, to hike on, I can only do it mincingly with little twinkletoe steps like Babe Ruth, twisting footsteps every way I can think of not to press too hard on any particular blister—So that the tourists (lessening now as the sun starts to go down) can now plainly see that

there's a man on the highway limping under a huge pack and asking
for a ride, but still they're afraid he may be the Hollywood hitch hiker
with the hidden gun and besides he's got a rucksack on his back as
tho he'd just escaped from the war in Cuba—Or's got dismembered
bodies in the bag anyway—But as I say I dont blame them.

The only car that passes that might have given me a ride is going
in the wrong direction, down to Sur, and it's a rattly old car of some
kind with a big bearded "South Coast Is the Lonely Coast" folksinger
in it waving at me but finally a little truck pulls up and waits for me
50 yards ahead and I limprun that distance on daggers in my feet—
It's a guy with a dog—He'll drive me to the next gas station, then he
turns off—But when he learns about my feet he takes me clear to the
bus station in Monterey—Just as a gesture of kindness—No particular reason, and I've made no particular plea about my feet, just mentioned it.

I offer to buy him a beer but he's going on home for supper so I go
into the bus station and clean up and change and pack things away,
stow the bag in the locker, buy the bus ticket, and go limping quietly
in the blue fog streets of Monterey evening feeling light as feather and
happy as a millionaire—The last time I ever hitch hiked—And NO
RIDES a sign.

11

THE NEXT SIGN IS in Frisco itself where after a night of perfect sleep in an old skid row hotel room I go to see Monsanto at his City Lights bookstore and he's smiling and glad to see me, says "We were coming out to see you next weekend you should have waited," but there's something else in his expression—When we're alone he says "Your mother wrote and said your cat is dead."

Ordinarily the death of a cat means little to most men, a lot to fewer men, but to me, and that cat, it was exactly and no lie and sincerely like the death of my little brother—I loved Tyke with all my heart, he was my baby who as a kitten just slept in the palm of my hand with his little head hanging down, or just purring, for hours, just as long as I held him that way, walking or sitting—He was like a floppy fur wrap around my wrist, I just twist him around my wrist or drape him and he just purred and purred and even when he got big I still held him that way, I could even hold this big cat in both hands with my arms outstretched right over my head and he'd just purr, he had complete confidence in me—And when I'd left New York to come to my retreat in the woods I'd carefully kissed him and instructed him to wait for me, "*Attends pour mué kitigingoo*"—But my mother said in the letter he had died the NIGHT AFTER I LEFT!—But maybe you'll understand me by seeing for yourself by reading the letter:-

"Sunday July 20, 1960, Dear Son, I'm afraid you wont like my letter because I only have sad news for you right now. I really dont know how to tell you this but Brace up Honey. I'm going through hell myself. Little Tyke is *gone*. Saturday all day he was fine and seemed to pick up strength, but late at night I was watching T.V. a late movie. Just about 1:30 A.M. when he started belching and throwing up. I went to him and tried to fix him up but to no *availe*. He was shivering like he was cold so I rapped him up in a Blanket then he started to throw up all over me. And that was the last of him. Needless to say how I

feel and what I went through. I stayed up till 'day *Break*' and did all
I could to revive him but it was useless. I realized at 4 A.M. he was
gone so at six I wrapped him up good in a clean blanket—and at 7
A.M. went out to dig his grave. I never did anything in my whole life
so heart breaking as to bury my beloved little Tyke who was as human
as you and I. I buried him under the Honeysuckle vines, the corner, of
the fence. I just cant sleep or eat. I keep looking and hoping to see him
come through the cellar door calling *Ma Wow*. I'm just plain sick and
the weirdest thing happened when I buried Tyke, all the black Birds I
fed all Winter seemed to have known what was going on. Honest Son
this is no lies. There was lots and lots of *em* flying over my head and
chirping, and settling on the fence, for a whole hour after Tyke was
laid to rest—that's something I'll never forget—I wish I had a camera
at the time but God and Me knows it and saw it. Now Honey I know
this is going to hurt you but I had to tell you somehow. . . I'm so sick
not physically but heart sick. . . I just cant believe or realize that my
Beautiful little Tyke is no more—and that I wont be seeing him come
through his little "Shanty" or Walking through the green grass. . . .
P.S. I've got to dismantle Tyke's shanty, I just cant go out there and see
it empty—as is. Well Honey, write soon again and be kind to yourself.
Pray the real "God"—Your old Mom X X X X XX."

So when Monsanto told me the news and I was sitting there *smiling*
with happiness the way all people feel when they come out of a long
solitude either in the woods or in a hospital bed, bang, my heart sank,
it sank in fact with the same strange idiotic helplessness as when I
took the unfortunate deep breath on the seashore—All the premoni-
tions tying in together.

Monsanto sees that I'm terribly sad, he sees my little smile (the smile
that came over me in Monterey just so glad to be back in the world
after the solitudes and I'd walked around the streets just bemusedly
Mona Lisa'ing at the sight of everything)—He sees now how that
smile has slowly melted away into a mawk of chagrin—Of course he
cant know since I didnt tell him and hardly wanta tell it now, that my
relationship with my cat and the other previous cats has always been a
little dotty: some kind of psychological identification of the cats with
my dead brother Gerard who'd taught me to love cats when I was 3

and 4 and we used to lie on the floor on our bellies and watch them lap up milk—The death of "little brother" Tyke indeed—Monsanto seeing me so downcast says "Maybe you oughta go back to the cabin for a few more weeks—or are you just gonna get drunk again"—"I'm gonna get drunk yes"—Because anyway there are so many things brewing, everybody's waiting, I've been daydreaming a thousand wild parties in the woods—In fact it's fortunate I've heard of the death of Tyke in my favorite exciting city of San Francisco, if I had been home when he died I might have gone mad in a different way but tho I now ran out to get drunk with the boys and still once in a while that funny little smile of joy came back as I drank, and melted away again because now the smile itself was a reminder of death, the news made me go mad anyway at the end of the three week binge, creeping up on me finally on that terrible day of St. Carolyn By The Sea as I can also call it—All, all confusing till I explain.

Meanwhile anyway poor Monsanto a man of letters wants to enjoy big news swappings with me about writing and what everybody's doing, and then Fagan comes into the store (downstairs to Monsanto's old rolltop desk making me also feel chagrin because it always was the ambition of my youth to end up a kind of literary businessman with a rolltop desk, combining my father image with the image of myself as a writer, which Monsanto without even thinking about it has accomplished at the drop of a hat)—Monsanto with his husky shoulders, big blue eyes, twinkling rosy skin, that perpetual smile of his that earned him the name Smiler in college and a smile you often wondered "Is it real?" until you realized if Monsanto should ever stop using that smile how could the world go on anyway—It was that kind of smile too inseparable from him to be believably allowed to dis-appear—Words words words but he is a grand guy as I'll show and now with real manly sympathy he really felt I should not go on big binges if I felt so bad, "At any rate," sez he, "you can go back a little later huh"—"Okay Lorry"—"Did you write anything?"—"I wrote the sounds of the sea, I'll tell you all about it—It was the most happy three weeks of my life dammit and now this has to happen, poor little Tyke—You should have seen him a big beautiful yellow Persian the kind they call calico"—"Well you still have my dog Homer, and how

was Alf out there?"—"Alf the Sacred Burro, he ha, he stands in groves
of trees in the afternoon suddenly you see him it's almost scarey, but
I fed him apples and shredded wheat and everything" (and animals
are so sad and patient I thought as I remembered Tyke's eyes and Alf's
eyes, ah death, and to think this strange scandalous death comes also
to human beings, yea to Smiler even, poor Smiler, and poor Homer
his dog, and all of us)—I'm also depressed because I know how horrible my mother now feels all alone without her little chum in the house
back there 3 thousand miles (and indeed by Jesus it turns out later
some silly beatniks trying to see me broke the windowpane in the
front door trying to get in and scared her so much she barricaded the
door with furniture all the rest of that summer).

But there's old Ben Fagan puffing and chuckling over his pipe so
what the hell, why bother grownup men and poets at that with your
own troubles—So Ben and I and his chum Jonesy also a chuckly pipe-
smoker go out to the bar (Mike's Place) and sip a few beers, at first I
vow I'm not going to get drunk after all, we even go out to the park
to have a long talk in the warm sun that always turns to delightful
cool foggy dusk in that town of towns—We're sitting in the park of
the big Italian white church watching kids play and people go by, for
some reason I'm bemused by the sight of a blonde woman hurrying
somewhere "Where's she going? does she have a secret sailor lover?
is she only going to finish her typing afterhours in the office? what
if we knew Ben what every one of these people goin by is headed for,
some door, some restaurant, some secret romance"—"You sound like
you stored up a lot of energy and innerest in life in those woods"—
And Ben knows that for sure because he's been months in the wil-
derness too, alone—Old Ben, much thinner than he used to be in our
madder Dharma Bum days of 5 years ago, a little gaunt in fact, but
still the same old Ben who stays up late at night chuckling over the
Lankavatara Scripture and writing poems about raindrops—And he
knows me very well, he knows I'll get drunk tonight and for weeks
on end just on general principles and that a day will come in a few
weeks when I'll be so exhausted I wont be able to talk to anybody
and he'll come and visit me and just silently at my side be puffing
his pipe, as I sleep—The kind of guy he is—I trying to explain about

Tyke to him but some people are cat lovers and some aint, tho Ben always has a little kitty around his pad—His pad usually has a straw rug on the floor, with a pillow 'pon which he sits crosslegged, by a smoking teapot, his bookshelves full of Stein and Pound and Wallace Stevens—A strange quiet poet who was only beginning to be recognized as a big rosy secret sage (one of his lines "When I leave town all my friends go back on the sauce")—And I'm on my way to the sauce right now.

Because anyway old Dave Wain is back and Dave I can see him rubbing his hands in anticipation of another big wild binge with me like we had the year before when he drove me back to New York from the west coast, with George Baso the little Japanese Zen master hepcat sitting crosslegged on the back mattress of Dave's jeepster (Willie the Jeep), a terrific trip through Las Vegas, St. Louis, stopping off at expensive motels and drinking nothing but the best Scotch out of the bottle all the way—And what better way to go back to New York, I could have blown 190 dollars on an airplane—And Dave's never met the great Cody and will be looking forward to that—So me and Ben leave the park and slowly walk to the bar on Columbus Street and I order my first double bourbon and gingerale.

The lights are twinkling on outside in that fantastic toy street, I can feel the joy rise in my soul—I now remember Big Sur with a clear piercing love and agony and even the death of Tyke fits in with everything but I dont realize the enormity of what's yet to come—We call up Dave Wain who's back from Reno and he comes blattin down to the bar in his jeepster driving that marvelous way he does (once he was a cab-driver) talking all the time and never making a mistake, in fact as good a driver as Cody altho I cant imagine anybody being that good and asked Cody about it the next day—But old jealous drivers always point out faults and complain, "Ah well that Dave Wain of yours doesnt takes his curves right, he eases up and sometimes even pokes the brake a little instead of just ridin that old curve around on increased power, man you gotta *work* those curves"—Obvious at this time now, by the way and parenthetically, that there's so much to tell about the fateful following three weeks it's hardly possible to find anyplace to begin.

Like life, actually—And how multiple it all is!—"And what happened to little old George Baso, boy?"—"Little old George Baso is
probably dyin of T.B. in a hospital outsida Tulare"—"Gee, Dave, we
gotta go see him"—"Yessir, let's do that tomorrow"—As usual Dave
has no money whatever but that doesnt bother me at all, I've got
plenty, I go out the following day and cash 500 dollars worth of travelers checks just so's me and old Dave can really have a good time—
Dave likes good food and drink and so do I—But he's got this young
kid he brought back from Reno called Ron Blake who is a goodlooking teenager with blond hair who wants to be a sensational new Chet
Baker singer and comes on with that tiresome hipster approach that
was natural 5 or 10 and even 25 years ago but now in 1960 is a pose,
in fact I dug him as a con man conning Dave (tho for what, I dont
know)—But Dave Wain that lean rangy red head Welchman with
his penchant for going off in Willie to fish in the Rogue River up in
Oregon where he knows an abandoned mining camp, or for blattin
around the desert roads, for suddenly reappearing in town to get
drunk, and a marvelous poet himself, has that certain something that
young hip teenagers probably wanta imitate—For one thing is one of
the world's best talkers, and funny too—As I'll show—It was he and
George Baso who hit on the fantastically simple truth that everybody
in America was walking around with a dirty behind, but everybody,
because the ancient ritual of washing with water after the toilet had
not occurred in all the modern antisepticsm—Says Dave "People in
America have all these racks of drycleaned clothes like you say on
their trips, they spatter Eau de Cologne all over themselves, they wear
Ban and Aid or whatever it is under their armpits, they get aghast
to see a spot on a shirt or a dress, they probably change underwear
and socks maybe even twice a day, they go around all puffed up and
insolent thinking themselves the cleanest people on earth and they're
walkin around with dirty azzoles—Isnt that amazing? give me a little
nip on that tit" he says reaching for my drink so I order two more, I've
been engrossed, Dave can order all the drinks he wants anytime, "The
President of the United States, the big ministers of state, the great
bishops and shmishops and big shots everywhere, down to the lowest
factory worker with all his fierce pride, movie stars, executives and

great engineers and presidents of law firms and advertising firms with silk shirts and neckties and great expensive traveling cases in which they place these various expensive English imported hair brushes and shaving gear and pomades and perfumes are all walkin around with dirty azzoles! All you gotta do is simply wash yourself with soap and water! it hasnt occurred to anybody in America at all! it's one of the funniest things I've ever heard of! dont you think it's marvelous that we're being called filthy unwashed beatniks but we're the only ones walkin around with clean azzoles?"—The whole azzole shot in fact had spread swiftly and everybody I knew and Dave knew from coast to coast had embarked on this great crusade which I must say is a good one—In fact in Big Sur I'd instituted a shelf in Monsanto's outhouse where the soap must be kept and everyone had to bring a can of water there on each trip—Monsanto hadnt heard about it yet, "Do you realize that until we tell poor Lorenzo Monsanto the famous writer that he is walking around with a dirty azzole he will be doing just that?"—"Let's go tell him right now!"—"Why of course if we wait another minute . . . and besides do you know what it *does* to people to walk around with a dirty azzole? it leaves a great yawning guilt that they cant understand all day, they go to work all cleaned up in the morning and you can smell all that freshly laundered clothes and Eau de Cologne in the commute train yet there's something gnawing at them, something's wrong, they know something's wrong they dont know just what!"—We rush to tell Monsanto at once in the book store around the corner.

By now we're beginning to feel great—Fagan has retired saying typically "Okay you guys go ahead and get drunk, I'm goin home and spend a quiet evening in a hot bath with a book"—"Home" is also where Dave Wain and Ron Blake live—It's an old roominghouse of four stories on the edge of the Negro district of San Francisco where Dave, Ben, Jonesy, a painter called Lanny Meadows, a mad French Canadian drinker called Pascal and a Negro called Johnson all live in different rooms with their clutter of rucksacks and floor mattresses and books and gear, each one taking turns one day a week to go out and do all the shopping and come back and cook up a big communal dinner in the kitchen—All ten or twelve of them sharing the rent, and

with that rotation of dinner, they end up living comfortable lives with
wild parties and girls rushing in, people bringing bottles, all at about
a minimum of seven dollars a week say—It's a wonderful place but
at the same time a little maddening, in fact a whole lot maddening
because the painter Lanny Meadows loves music and has installed his
Hi Fi speaker in the kitchen altho he applies the records in a back
room so the daily cook may be concentrating on his Mulligan stew
and all of a sudden Stravinski's dinosaurs start dinning overhead—
And at night there are bottlecrashing parties usually supervised by
wild Pascal who is a sweet kid but crazy when he drinks—A regular
nuthouse actually and just exactly the image of what the journalists
want to say about the Beat Generation nevertheless a harmless and
pleasant arrangement for young bachelors and a good idea in the
long run—Because you can rush into any room and find the expert,
like say Ben's room and ask "Hey what did Bodhidharma say to the
Second Patriarch?"—"He said go fuck yourself, make your mind like
a wall, dont pant after outside activities and dont bug me with your
outside plans"—"So the guy goes out and stands on his head in the
snow?"—"No that was Fubar"—Or you go runnin into Dave Wain's
room and there he is sitting crosslegged on his mattress on the floor
reading Jane Austen, you ask "What's the best way to make beef
Stroganoff?"—"Beef Stroganoff is very simple, 'taint nothin but a good
well cooked beef and onion stew that you let cool afterwards then you
throw in mushrooms and lotsa sour cream, I'll come down and show
way soon's I finish this chapter in this marvelous novel, I wanta find
out what happens next"—Or you go into the Negro's room and ask if
you can borrow his tape recorder because right at the moment some
funny things are being said in the kitchen by Duluoz and McLear
and Monsanto and some newspaperman—Because the kitchen was
also the main talking room where everybody sat in a clutter of dishes
and ashtrays and all kinds of visitors came—The year before a beautiful 16 year old Japanese girl had come there just to interview me,
for instance, but chaperoned by a Chinese painter—The phone rang
consistently—Even wild Negro hepcats from around the corner came
in with bottles (Edward Kool and several others)—There was Zen,
jazz, booze, pot and all the works but it was somehow obviated (as a

supposedly degenerate idea) by the sight of a 'beatnik' carefully painting the wall of his room and clean white with nice little red borders
around the door and windowframes—Or someone is sweeping out
the livingroom. Itinerant visitors like me or Ron Blake always had an
extra mattress to sleep on.

12

BUT DAVE IS ANXIOUS and so am I to see great Cody who is always the major part of my reason for journeying to the west coast so we call him up at Los Gatos 50 miles away down the Santa Clara Valley and I hear his dear sad voice saying "Been waitin for ya old buddy, come on down right away, but I'll be goin to work at midnight so hurry up and you can visit me at work soon's the boss leaves round two and I'll show you my new job of tire recappin and see if you cant bring a little somethin like a girl or sumptin, just kiddin, come on down pal—"

So there's old Willie waiting for us down on the street parked across from the little pleasant Japanese liquor store where as usual, according to our ritual, I run and get Pernod or Scotch or anything good while Dave wheels around to pick me up at the store door, and I get in the front seat right at Dave's right where I belong all the time like old Honored Samuel Johnson while everybody else that wants to come along has to scramble back there on the mattress (a full mattress, the seats are out) and squat there or lie down there and also generally keep silent because when Dave's got the wheel of Willie in his hand and I've got the bottle in mine and we're off on a trip the talking all comes from the front seat—"By God" yells Dave all glad again "it's just like old times Jack, gee old Willie's been sad for ya, waitin for ya to come back—So now I'm gonna show ya how old Willie's even improved with age, had him reconditioned in Reno last month, here he goes, are you ready Willie?" and off we go and the beauty of it all this particular summer is that the front right seat is broken and just rocks back and forth gently to every one of Dave's driving moves— It's like sitting in a rocking chair on a porch only this is a moving porch and a porch to talk on at that—And insteada watching old men pitch horseshoes from this here talking porch it's all that fine white clean line in the middle of the road as we go flying like birds over the Harrison ramps and whatnot Dave always uses to sneak out of

Frisco real fast and avoid all the traffic—Soon we're set straight and pointed head on down beautiful fourlane Bayshore Highway to that lovely Santa Clara Valley—But I'm amazed that after only a few years the damn thing no longer has prune fields and vast beet fields like at Lawrence when I was a brakeman on the Southern Pacific and even after, it's one long row of houses right down the line 50 miles to San Jose like a great monstrous Los Angeles beginning to grow south of Frisco.

At first it's beautiful to just watch that white line reel in to Willie's snout but when I start looking around out the window there's just endless housing tracts and new blue factories everywhere—Sez Dave "Yes that's right, the population explosion is gonna cover every bit of backyard dirt in America someday in fact they'll even have to start piling up friggin levels of houses and others over that like your city-CityCITY till the houses reach a hundred miles in the air in all directions of the map and people looking at the earth from another planet with super telescopes will see a prickly ball hangin in space—It's like real horrible when you come to think of it, even us with all our fancy talks, shit man it's all millions of people and events piling up almost unimaginable now, like raving babboons we'll all be piled on top of each other or one another or whatever you're sposed to say—Hundreds of millions of hungry mouths raving for more more more—And the sadness of it all is that the world hasnt any chance to produce say a writer whose life could really actually touch all this life in every detail like you always say, some writer who could bring you sobbing thru the bed fuckin bedcribs of the moon to see it all even unto the goddamned last gory detail of some dismal robbery of the heart at dawn when no one cares like Sinatra sings" ("When no one cares," he sings in his low baritone but resumes):—"Some strict sweeper sweeping it all up, I mean the incredible helplessness I felt Jack when Céline ended his Journey To The End Of The Night by pissing in the Seine River at dawn there I am thinkin my God there's probably somebody pissing in the Trenton River at dawn right now, the Danube, the Ganges, the frozen Obi, the Yellow, the Paraña, the Willamette, the Merrimac in Missouri too, the Missouri itself, the Yuma, the Amazon, the Thames, the Po, the so and so, it's so friggin endless it's like poems endless everywhere and no one knows any bettern old Buddha you know where he says it's like "There are immeasurable star misty aeons of universes more numerous than the sands in all the galaxies, multiplied by a billion lightyears of multiplication, in fact if I were to go on you'd be scared and couldnt comprehend and you'd despair so much you'd drop dead,' that's what he just about said in one of those sutras—Macrocosms and microcosms and chillicosms and microbes and finally you got all these marvelous books a man aint even got time to read em all, what you gonna do in this already piled up multiple world when you have to think of the Book of Songs, Faulkner, César Birotteau, Shakespeare, Satyricons, Dantes, in fact long stories guys tell you in bars, in fact the sutras themselves, Sir Philip Sidney, Sterne, Ibn El Arabi, the copious Lope de Vega and the uncopious goddamn Cervantes, shoo, then there's all those Catulluses and Davids and radio listening skid row sages to contend with because they've all got a million stories too and you too Ron Blake in the backseat shut up! down to everything which is so much that it is of necessity dont you think NOthing anyway, huh?" (expressing exactly the way I feel, of course).

And to corroborate all that about the too-much-ness of the world, in fact, there's Stanley Popovich also in the back mattress next to Ron, Stanley Popovich of New York suddenly arrived in San Francisco with Jamie his Italian beauty girl but's going to leave her in a few days to go work for the circus, a big tough Yugoslav kid who ran the Seven Arts Gallery in New York with big bearded beatnik readings but now comes the circus and a whole big on-the-road of his own—It's too much, in fact right this minute he's started telling us about circus work—On top of all that old Cody is up ahead with HIS thousand stories—We all agree it's too big to keep up with, that we're surrounded by life, that we'll never understand it, so we center it all in by swigging Scotch from the bottle and when it's empty I run out of the car and buy another one, period.

13

BUT ON THE WAY to Cody's my madness already began to manifest itself in a stranger way, another one of those signposts of something wrong I mentioned a ways back: I thought I saw a flying saucer in the sky over Los Gatos—From five miles away—I look and I see this thing flying along and mention it to Dave who takes one brief look and says "Ah it's only the top of a radio tower"—It reminds me of the time I took a mescaline pill and thought an airplane was a flying saucer (a strange story this, a man has to be crazy to write it anyway).

But there's old Cody in the livingroom of his fine ranchito home sittin over his chess set pondering a problem and right by the fresh woodfire in the fireplace his wife's set out because she knows I love fireplaces—She a good friend of mine too—The kids are sleeping in the back, it's about eleven, and good old Cody shakes my hand again—Havent seen him for several years because mainly he's just spent two years in San Quentin on a stupid charge of possession of marijuana—He was on his way to work on the railroad one night and was short on time and his driving license had been already revoked for speeding so he saw two bearded bluejeaned beatniks parked, asked them to trade a quick ride to work at the railroad station for two sticks of tea, they complied and arrested him—They were disguised police-men—For this great crime he spent two years in San Quentin in the same cell with a murderous gunman—His job was sweeping out the cotton mill room—I expect him to be all bitter and out of his head because of this but strangely and magnificently he's become quieter, more radiant, more patient, manly, more friendly even—And tho the wild frenzies of his old road days with me have banked down he still has the same taut eager face and supple muscles and looks like he's ready to go anytime—But actually loves his home (paid for by rail-road insurance when he broke his leg trying to stop a boxcar from crashing), loves his wife in a way tho they fight some, loves his kids

and especially his little son Timmy John partly named after me—Poor
old, good old Cody sittin there with his chess set, wants immediately
to challenge somebody to a chess game but only has an hour to talk to
us before he goes to work supporting the family by rushing out and
pushing his Nash Rambler down the quiet Los Gatos suburb street,
jumping in, starting the motor, in fact his only complaint is that the
Nash wont start without a push—No bitter complaints about society
whatever from this grand and ideal man who really loves me more-
over as if I deserved it, but I'm bursting to explain everything to him,
not even Big Sur but the past several years, but there's no chance with
everybody yakking—And in fact I can see in Cody's eyes that he can
see in my own eyes the regret we both feel that recently we havent had
chances to talk whatever, like we used to do driving across America
and back in the old road days, too many people now want to talk to us
and tell us *their* stories, we've been hemmed in and surrounded and
outnumbered—The circle's closed in on the old heroes of the night—
But he says "However you guys, come on down round 'bout one when
the boss leaves and watch me work and keep me company awhile
before you go back to the City"—I can see Dave Wain really loves
him at once, and Stanley Popovich too who's come along on this trip
just to meet the fabled "Dean Moriarty"—The name I give Cody in
"On the Road"—But O, it breaks my heart to see he's lost his beloved
job on the railroad and after all the seniority he'd piled up since 1948
and now is reduced to tire recapping and dreary parole visits—All for
two sticks of wild loco weed that grows by itself in Texas because God
wanted it—

And there over the bookshelf is the old photo of me and Cody arm
in arm in the early days on a sunny street—

I rush to explain to Cody what happened the year before when his
religious advisor at the prison had invited me to come to San Quentin
to lecture the religious class—Dave Wain was supposed to drive me
and wait outside the prison walls as I'd go in there alone, probably
with a pepup nip bottle hidden in my coat (I hoped) and I'd be led by
big guards to the lecture room of the prison and there would be sitting
a hundred or so cons including Cody probably all proud in the front
row—And I would begin by telling them I had been in jail myself once

and that I had no right nevertheless to lecture them on religion—But they're all lonely prisoners and dont care what I talk about—The whole thing arranged, in any case, and on the big morning I wake up instead dead drunk on a floor, it's already noon and too late, Dave Wain is on the floor also, Willie's parked outside to take us to Quentin for the lecture but it's too late—But now Cody says "It's alright old buddy I understand"—Altho our friend Irwin had done it, lectured there, but Irwin can do all sorta things like that being more social than I am and capable of going in there as he did and reading his wildest poems which set the prison yard humming with excitement tho I think he shouldna done it after all because I say just to show up for any reason except visiting inside a prison is still SIGNIFYING—And I tell this to Cody who ponders a chess problem and says "Drinkin again, hey?" (if there's anything he hates is to see me drink).

We help him push his Nash down the street, then drink awhile and talk with Evelyn a beautiful blonde woman that young Ron Blake wants and even Dave Wain wants but she's got her mind on other things and taking care of the children who have to go to school and dancing classes in the morning and hardly gets a word in edgewise anyway as we all yak and yell like fools to impress her tho all she really wants is to be alone with me to talk about Cody and his latest soul.

Which includes the fact of Billie Dabney his mistress who has threatened to take Cody away completely from Evelyn, as I'll show later.

So we do go out to the San Jose highway to watch Cody recap tires—There he is wearing goggles working like Vulcan at his forge, throwing tires all over the place with fantastic strength, the good ones high up on a pile, "This one's no good" down on another, bing, bang, talking all the time a long fantastic lecture on tire recapping which has Dave Wain marvel with amazement—("My God he can do all that and even explain while he's doing it")—But I just mention in connection with the fact that Dave Wain now realizes why I've always loved Cody—Expecting to see a bitter ex con he sees instead a martyr of the American Night in goggles in some dreary tire shop at 2 A.M. making fellows laugh with joy with his funny explanations yet at the same time to a T performing every bit of the work he's being paid for—Rushing up and ripping tires off car wheels with a jicklo, clang, throwing it on the machine, starting up big roaring steams but yelling explanations over that, darting, bending, flinging, flaying, till Dave Wain said he thought he was going to die laughing or crying right there on the spot.

So we drive back to town and go to the mad boarding-house to drink some more and I pass out dead drunk on the floor as usual in that house, waking up in the morning groaning far from my clean cot on the porch in Big Sur—No bluejays yakking for me to wake up any more, no gurgling creek, I'm back in the grooky city and I'm trapped.

14

INSTEAD THERE'S THE SOUND of bottles crashing in the livingroom where poor Lex Pascal is holding forth yelling, it reminds of the time a year ago when Jarry Wagner's future wife got sore at Lex and threw a half gallonfull of tokay across the room and hooked him right across the eye, thereupon sailing to Japan to marry Jarry in a big Zen ceremony that made coast to coast papers but all old Lex's got is a cut which I try to fix in the bathroom upstairs saying "Hey, that cut's already stopped bleeding, you'll be alright Lex"—"I'm French Canadian too" he says proudly and when Dave and I and George Baso get ready to drive back to New York he gives me a St. Christopher medal as a goingaway gift—Lex the kind of guy shouldnt really be living in this wild beat boardinghouse, should hide on a ranch somewhere, powerful, goodlooking, full of crazy desire for women and booze and never enough of either—So as the bottles crash again and the Hi Fi's playing Beethoven's Solemn Mass I fall asleep on the floor.

Waking up the next morning groaning of course, but this is the big day when we're going to go visit poor George Baso at the TB hospital in the Valley—Dave perks me up right away bringing coffee or wine optional—I'm on Ben Fagan's floor somehow, apparently I've harangued him till dawn about Buddhism—some Buddhist.

Complicated already but now suddenly appears Joey Rosenberg a strange young kid from Oregon with a full beard and his hair growing right down to his neck like Raul Castro, once the California High School high jump champ who was only about 5 foot 6 but had made the incredible leap of six foot nine over the bar! and shows his highjump ability too by the way he dances around on light feet—A strange athlete who's suddenly decided instead to become some sort of beat Jesus and in fact you see perfect purity and sincerity in his young blue eyes—In fact his eyes are so pure you dont notice the crazy hair and beard, and also he's wearing ragged but strangely elegant clothing

("One of the first of the new Beat Dandies," McLear told me a few days
later, "did you hear about that? there's a new strange underground
group of beatniks or whatever who wear special smooth dandy clothes
even tho it may just be a jean jacket with shino slacks they'll always
have strange beautiful shoes or shirts, or turn around and wear fancy
pants unpressed acourse but with torn sneakers")—Joey is wearing
something like brown soft garments like a tunic or something and
his shoes look like Las Vegas sports shoes—The moment he sees my
battered blue little sneakers that I'd used at Big Sur when my feet go
sore, that is in case my feet got sore on a rocky hike, he wants them
for himself, he wants to swap the snazzy Las Vegas sports shoes (pale
leather, untooled) for my silly little tightfitting tho perfect sneakers
that in fact I was wearing because the Monterey hike blisters were
still hurting me—So we swap—And I ask Dave Wain about him:
Dave says: "He's one of the really strangest sweetest guys I've ever
known, showed up about a week ago I hear tell, they asked him what
he wanted to do and never answers, just smiles—He just sorta wants
to dig everything and just watch and enjoy and say nothing particular
about it—If someone's to ask him 'Let's drive to New York' he'd jump
right for it without a word—On a sort of a pilgrimage, see, with all
that youth, us old fucks oughta take a lesson from him, in faith too, he
has faith, I can see it in his eyes, he has faith in any direction he may
take with anyone just like Christ I guess."

It's strange that in a later revery I imagined myself walking across a
field to find the strange gang of pilgrims in Arkansas and Dave Wain
was sitting there saying "Shhh, He's sleeping," "He" being Joey and all
the disciples are following him on a march to New York after which
they expect to keep going walking on water to the other shore—But of
course (in my revery even) I scoff and dont believe it (a kind of story
daydreaming I often do) but in the morning when I look into Joey
Rosenberg's eyes I instantly realize it IS Him, Jesus, because anyone
(according to the rules of my revery) who looks into those eyes is
instantly convinced and converted—So the revery continues into a
long farfetched story ending with thinking I.B.M. machines trying to
destroy this "Second Coming" etc. (but also, in reality, a few months
later I threw away his shoes in the ashcan back home because I felt

they had brought me bad luck and wishing I'd kept my blue sneakers with the little holes in the toes!)

So anyway we get Joey and Ron Blake who's always following Dave and go off to see Monsanto at the store, our usual ritual, then across the corner to Mike's Place where we start off the 10 A.M. with food, drink and a few games of pool at the tables along the bar—Joey winning the game and a stranger poolshark you never saw with his long Biblical hair bending to slide the cue stick smoothly through completely professionally competent fingerstance and smashing home long straight drives, like seeing Jesus shoot pool of course—And meanwhile all the food these poor starved kids all three of them do pack in and eat!— It's not every day they're with a drunken novelist with hundreds of dollars to splurge on them, they order everything, spaghetti, follow that up with Jumbo Hamburgers, follow that up with ice cream and pie and puddings, Dave Wain has a huge appetite anyway but adds Manhattans and Martinis to the side of his plate—I'm just wailing away on my old fatal double bourbons and gingerale and I'll be sorry in a few days.

Any drinker knows how the process works: the first day you get drunk is okay, the morning after means a big head but so you can kill that easy with a few more drinks and a meal, but if you pass up the meal and go on to another night's drunk, and wake up to keep the toot going, and continue on to the fourth day, there'll come one day when the drinks wont take effect because you're chemically overloaded and you'll have to sleep it off but cant sleep any more because it was alcohol itself that made you sleep those last five nights, so delirium sets in—Sleeplessness, sweat, trembling, a groaning feeling of weakness where your arms are numb and useless, nightmares, (nightmares of death) . . . well, there's more of that up later.

About noon which is now the peak of a golden blurry new day for me we pick up Dave's girl Romana Swartz a big Rumanian monster beauty of some kind (I mean with big purple eyes and very tall and big but Mae West big), Dave whispers in my ear "You oughta see her walking around that Zen-East House in those purple panties of hers, nothing else on, there's one married guy lives there who goes crazy every time she goes down the hall tho I dont blame him, would you? she's not trying to entice him or anybody she's just a nudist, she believe in nudism and bygod she's going to practice it!" (the Zen-East house being another sort of boardinghouse but this one for all kinds of married people and single and some small bohemian type families all races studying Subud or something, I never was there)—She's a big beautiful brunette anyway in the line of taste you might attribute to every slaky hungry sex slave in the world but also intelligent, well read, writes poetry, is a Zen student, knows everything, is in fact just simply a big healthy Rumanian Jewess who wants to marry a good hardy man and go live on a farm in the valley, that's it—

The T.B. hospital is about two hours away through Tracy and down the San Joaquin Valley, Dave drives beautiful with Romana between us and me holding the bottle again, it's bright beautiful California sunshine and prune orchards out there zipping by—It's always fun to have a good driver and a bottle and dark glasses on a fine sunny afternoon going somewhere interesting, and all the good conversation as I said—Ron and Joey are on the back mattress sitting crosslegged just like poor George Baso had sat on that trip last year from Frisco to New York.

But the main thing I'd liked at once about that Japanese kid was what he told me the first night I met him in that crazy kitchen of the Buchanan Street house: from midnight to 6 A.M. in his slow methodical voice he gave me his own tremendous version of the Life of Buddha beginning with infancy and right down to the end—George's theory (he has many theories and has actually run meditation classes with bells, just really a serious young lay priest of Japanese Buddhism when all is said and done) is that Buddha did not reject amorous love life with his wife and with his harem girls because he was sexually disinterested but on the contrary had been taught in the highest arts of lovemaking and eroticism possible in the India of that time, when great tomes like the Kama Sutra were in the process of being developed, tomes that give you instructions on every act, facet, approach, moment, trick, lick, lock, bing and bang and slurp of how to make love with another human being "male or female" insisted George: "He knew everything there is to know about all kinds of sex so that when he abandoned the world of pleasure to go be an ascetic in the forest everybody of course knew that he wasnt putting it all down out of ignorance—It served to make people of those times feel a marvelous respect for all his words—And he was just no simple Casanova with a few frigid affairs across the years, man he went all the way, he had ministers and special eunuchs and special women who taught him love, special virgins were brought to him, he was acquainted with every aspect of perversity and non perversity and as you know he was also a great archer, horseman, he was just completely trained in all the arts of living by his father's orders because his father wanted to make sure he'd NEVER leave the palace—They used every trick in the books to entice him to a life of pleasure and as you know they even had him happily married to a beautiful girl called Yasodhara and he had a son with her Rahula and he also had his harem which included dancing boys and everything in the books" then George would go into every detail of this knowledge, like "He knew that the phallus is held with the hand and moved inside the vagina with a rotary movement, but this was only the first of several variations where there is also the lowering down of the gal's hips so that the vulva you see recedes and the phallus is introduced with a fast quick movement like stinging of a wasp, or else the vulva is protruded by means of lifting up the hips high so that the member is buried with a sudden rush right to the basis, or then he can withdraw real teasing like, or concentrate on right or left side—And then he knew all the gestures, words, expressions, what to do with a flower, what not to do with a flower, how to drink the lip in all kinds of kissing or how to crush kiss or soft kiss, man he was a *genius* in the beginning" . . . and so on, George went all the way telling me this till 6 A.M. it being one of the most fantastic *Buddha Charitas* I'd ever heard ending with George's own perfect enunciation of the law of the Twelve Nirdanas whereby Buddha just logically disconnected all creation and laid it bare for what it was, under the Bo Tree, a chain of illusions—And on the trip to New York with Dave and me up front talking all the way poor George just sat there on the mattress for the most part very quiet and told us he was taking this trip to find out if HE was traveling to New York or just the CAR (Willie the Jeep) was traveling to New York or was it just the WHEELS were rolling, or the tires, or what—A Zen problem of some kind—So that when we'd see grain elevators on the Plains of Oklahoma George would say quietly "Well it seems to me that grain elevator is sorta waitin for the road to approach it" or he'd say suddenly "While you guys was talkin just then about how to mix a good Pernod Martini I just saw a white horse standing in an abandoned storefront"—In Las Vegas we'd taken a good motel room and gone out to play a little roulette, in St. Louis we'd gone to see the great bellies of the East St. Louis hootchy kootchy joints where three of the most marvelous young girls performed smiling directly at us as tho they knew all about George and his theories about erogenous Buddha (there sits the monarch observing the donzinggerls) and as tho they knew anyway all about Dave Wain who whenever he sees a beautiful girls says licking his lips "Yum Yum.". . .

But now George has T.B. and they tell me he may even die—Which adds to that darkness in my mind, all these DEATH things piling up suddenly—But I cant believe old Zen Master George is going to allow his body to die just now tho it looks like it when we pass through the lawn and come to a ward of beds and see him sitting dejected on the edge of his bed with his hair hanging over his brow where before it was always combed back—He's in a bathrobe and looks up at us almost displeased (but everybody is displeased by unexpected visits from friends or relatives in a hospital)—Nobody wants to be surprised on their hospital bad—He sighs and comes out to the warm lawn with us and the expression on his face says "Well ah so you've come to see me because I'm sick but what do you really want?" as tho all the old humorous courage of the year before has now given away to a profoundly deep Japanese skepticism like that of a Samurai warrior in a fit of suicidal depression (surprising me by its abject gloomy fearful frown).

15

I MEAN IT WAS like my first frightened realization of what to be Japanese really meant—To be Japanese and not to believe in life any more and to be gloomy like Beethoven yet to be Japanese in gloom, the gloom of Bashô behind it all, the huge thunderous scowl of Issa or of Shiki, kneeling in the frost with the bowed head like the bowed-head-oblivion of all the old horses of Japan long dust.

He sits there on the lawn bench looking down and when Dave asks him "Well you gonna be alright soon George" he says simply "I dont know"—He really means "I dont care"—And always warm and courteous with me he now hardly pays any attention to me—He's a little nervous because the other patients, G.I. vets, will see that he's received a visit from a bunch of ragged beatniks including Joey Rosenberg who is bouncing around the lawn looking at flowers with that bemused sincere smile—But little neat George, just 5 feet 5 and a few pounds over that and so clean, with his soft feathery hair like the hair of a child, his delicate hands, he just stares at the ground— His answers come like an old man's (he's only 30)—"I guess all the Dharma talk about everything is nothing is just sorta sinking in my bones," he concedes, which makes me shudder—(On the way Dave's been telling us to be ready because George's changed so)— But I try to keep things going, "Do you remember those dancing girls in St. Louis?"—"Yeh, whore candy" (he's referring to a piece of perfumed cotton one of the girls threw at us in her dance, which we tacked up later to a highway accident cross we'd yanked out of the ground one blood red sunset in Arizona, tacking this perfumed beautiful cotton right where the head of Christ was so that when we brought the cross to New York naturally we had everybody smelling it but George pointed out how beautiful we'd done all this subconsciously because the net result was that all the hepcats of Greenwich Village who came in to see us were picking up the cross and putting their heads (noses) to it)—But George doesnt care any more—And anyway it's time to leave.

But ah, as we're leaving and waving back at him and he's turned around tentatively to go into the hospital I linger behind the others and turn around several times to wave again—Finally I start to make a joke of it by ducking around a corner and peeking out and waving again—He ducks behind a bush and waves back—I dart to a bush and peek out—Suddenly we're two crazy hopeless sages goofing on a lawn—Finally as we part further and further and he comes closer to the door we are making elaborate gestures and down to the most infinitesimal like when he steps inside the door I wait till I see him sticking a finger out—So from around my corner I stick out a shoe— So from his door he sticks out an eye—So from my corner I stick out nothing but just yell "Wu!"—So from his door he sticks out nothing and says nothing—So I hide in the corner and do nothing—But suddenly I burst out and there HE is bursting out and we start waving gyrations and duck back to our hiding places—Then I pull a big one by simply walking away rapidly but suddenly I turn and wave again— He walking backwards and waving back—The further I go now also walking backwards the more I wave—Finally we're so far apart by about a hundred yards the game is almost impossible but we continue somehow—Finally I see a distant sad little Zen wave of hand—I jump up into the air and gyrate both arms—He does the same—He goes into the hospital but a moment later he's peeking out this time from the ward window!—I'm behind a tree trunk thumbing my nose at him—There's no end to it, in fact—The other kids are all back at the car wondering what's keeping me—What's keeping me is that I know George will get better and live and teach the joyful truth and George knows I know this, that's why he's playing the game with me, the magic game of glad freedom which is what Zen or for that matter the Japanese soul ultimately means I say, "And someday I will go to Japan with George" I tell myself after we've made our last little wave because I've heard the supper bell ring and seen the other patients rush for the chow line and knowing George's fantastic appetite wrapped in that little frail body I dont wanta hang him up tho he nevertheless does one last trick: He throws a glass of water out the window in a big froosh of water and I dont see him any more.

"Wotze mean by that?" I'm scratching my head going back to the car.

16

TO COMPLETE THIS CRAZY day at 3 o'clock in the morning here I am
sitting in a car being driven 100 miles an hour around the sleeping
streets and hills and waterfronts of San Francisco, Dave's gone off to
sleep with Romana and the others are passed out and this crazy nextdoor neighbor of the roominghouse (himself a Bohemian but also
a laborer, a housepainter who comes home with big muddy boots
and has his little boy living with him the wife has died)—I've been
in his pad listening to booming loud Stan Getz jazz on his Hi Fi
and happened to mention I thought Dave Wain and Cody Pomeray
were the two greatest drivers in the world—"What?" he yells, a big
blond husky kid with a strange fixed smile, "man I used to drive
the getaway car! come on down I'll show ya!"—So almost dawn
and here we are cuttin down Buchanan and around the corner on
screeching wheels and he opens her up, goes zipping towards a red
light so takes a sudden screeching left and goes up a hill fullblast,
when we come to the top of the hill I figger he'll pause awhile to see
what's over the top but he goes even faster and practically flies off
the hill and we head down one of those incredibly steep San Fran
streets with our snout pointed to the waters of the Bay and he steps
on the gas! we go sailing down a hundred m.p.h. to the bottom of the
hill where there's an intersection luckily with the light on green and
thru that we blast with just one little bump where the road crosses
and another bump where the street is dipping downhill again—We
come down to the waterfront and screech right—In a minute we're
soaring over the ramps around the Bridge entrance and before I can
gulp up a shot or two from my last late bottle we're already parked
back outside the pad on Buchanan—The greatest driver in the world
whoever he was and I never saw him again—Bruce something or
other—What a getaway.

17

I END UP GROANING drunk on the floor this time beside Dave's floor mattress forgetting that he's not even there.

But a strange thing happened that morning I remember now: before Cody's call from downvalley: I'm feeling hopelessly idiotically depressed again groaning to remember Tyke's dead and remembering that sinking beach but at the side of the radiator in the toilet lies a copy of Boswell's Johnson which we'd been discussing so happy in the car: I open to any page then one more page and start reading from the top left and suddenly I'm in an entirely perfect world again: old Doc Johnson and Boswell are visiting a castle in Scotland belonging to a deceased friend called Rorie More, they're drinking sherry by the great fireplace looking at the picture of Rorie on the wall, the widow of Rorie is there, Johnson suddenly says "Sir, here's what I would do to deal with the sword of Rorie More" (the portrait shows old Rorie with his Highlands flinger) "I'd get inside him with a dirk and stab him to my pleasure like an animal" and bleary with hangover I realize that if there was any way for Johnson to express his sorrow to the widow of Rorie More on the unfortunate circumstance of his death, this was the way—So pitiful, irrational, yet perfect—I rush down to the kitchen where Dave Wain and some others are already eating breakfast of sorts and start reading the whole thing to the lot of them—Jonesy looks at me askance over his pipe for being so literary so early in the morning but I'm not being literary at all—Again I see death, the death of Rorie More, but Johnson's response to death is ideal and so ideal I only wish old Johnson be sitting in the kitchen now—(Help! I'm thinking).

The call comes from Cody in Los Gatos that he lost his job tire recapping—"Because we were there last night?"—"No no something entirely different, he's gotta lay off some men because his mortgage is bleeding him and all that and some girl is tryna sue him for forging a check and all that, so man I've got to find another job but I have to pay the rent and everything's all fucked up down here, Oh old buddy how about, cant you, I plead or I dont plead, or honestly, Jack, ah, lend me a hundred dollars willya?"—"By God Cody I'll be right down and GIVE you a hundred dollars"—"You mean you'll really do that, listen just to lend to me is enough but if you insist, hm" (fluttering his eyelashes over the phone because he knows I mean it) "you old lover-boy you, how you gonna get down here there and give me that money there son and make my old heart glad"—"I'll have Dave drive me down"—"Okay I'll pay the rent with it right away and because it's now Friday, why, Thursday or whatever, that's right Thursday, why I dont have to be lookin for a new job till next Monday so you can stay here and we'll have a long weekend just goofin and talkin boy like we used to do, I can demolish you at chess or we can watch a baseball game" and in a whisper "and we can sneak into the City see and see my purty baby"—So I ask Dave Wain and yes he's ready to go anytime, he's just following me like I often follow people myself, and so off we go again.

And on the way we drop in on Monsanto at the bookstore and the idea suddenly comes to me for Dave and me and Cody to go to the cabin and spend a big quiet crazy weekend (how?) but when Monsanto hears this idea he'll come too, in fact he'll bring his little Chinese buddy Arthur Ma and we'll catch McLear at Santa Cruz and go visit Henry Miller and suddenly another big huge ball is begun.

So there's Willie waiting down on the street, I go to the store, buy the bottle, Dave wheels Willie around, Ron Blake and now Ben Fagan are on the back mattress, I'm sitting in my front seat rocking chair as now in broad afternoon we go blattin again down that Bay Shore highway to see old Cody and Monsanto's in back of us in his jeep with Arthur Ma, two jeeps now, and about to be two more as I'll show—Coming to Cody's in mid afternoon, his own house already filled with visitors (local Los Gatos literaries and all kinds of people the phone there ringing continually too) and Cody says to Evelyn "I'll just spend a couple days with Jack and the gang like the old days and look for a job Monday"—"Okay"—So we all go to a wonderful pizza restaurant in Los Gatos where the pizzas are piled an inch high with mushrooms and meat and anchovies or anything you want, I cash a travelers check at the supermarket, Cody takes the 100 in cash, gives it to Evelyn in the restaurant, and later that day the two jeeps resume down to Monterey and down that blasted road I walked on blistered feet back to the frightful bridge at Raton Canyon—And I'd thought I'd never see the place again. But now I was coming back loaded with observers. The sight of the canyon down there as we renegotiated the mountain road made me bite my lip with marvel and sadness.

18

IT'S AS FAMILIAR AS AN OLD FACE in an old photograph as tho I'm gone a million years from all that sun shaded brush on rocks and that heartless blue of the sea washing white on yellow sand, those rills of yellow arroyo running down mighty cliff shoulders, those distant blue meadows, that whole ponderous groaning upheaval so strange to see after the last several days of just looking at little faces and mouths of people—As tho nature had a Gargantuan leprous face of its own with broad nostrils and huge bags under its eyes and a mouth big enough to swallow five thousand jeepster stationwagons and ten thousand Dave Wains and Cody Pomerays without a sigh of reminiscence or regret—There it is, every sad contour of my valley, the gaps, the Mien Mo captop mountain again, the dreaming woods below our high shelved road, suddenly indeed the sight of poor Alf again far way grazing in the mid afternoon by the corral fence—And there's the creek bouncing along as tho nothing had ever happened elsewhere and even in the daytime somehow dark and hungry looking in its deeper tangled grass.

Cody's never seen this country before altho he's an old Californian by now, I can see he's very impressed and even glad he's come out on a little jaunt with the boys and with me and is seeing a grand sight—He's like a little boy again now for the first time in years because he's like let out of school, no job, the bills paid, nothing to do but gratefully amuse me, his eyes are shining—In fact ever since he's come out of San Quentin there's been something hauntedly boyish about him as tho prison walls had taken all the adult dark tenseness out of him—In fact every evening after supper in the cell he shared with the quiet gunman he'd bent his serious head to a daily letter or at least every-other-day letter full of philosophical and religious musings to his mistress Billie—And when you're in bed in jail after lights out and you're not sleepy there's ample time to just remember the world and indeed savor its sweetness if any (altho it's always sweet to remember it in jail tho harder in prison, as Genêt shows) with the result that he'd not only come to a chastisement of his bashing bitternesses (and of course it's always good to get away from alcohol and excessive smoking for two years) (and all that regular sleep) he was just like a kid again, but as I say that haunting kidlikeness I think all ex cons seem to have when they've just come out—In seeking to severely penalize criminals society by putting the criminals away behind safe walls actually provide them with the means of greater strength for future atrocities glorious and otherwise—"Well I'll be damned" he keeps saying as he sees those bluffs and cliffs and hanging vines and dead trees, "you mean to tell me you ben alone here for three weeks, why I wouldnt dare that . . . must be awful at night . . . looka that old mule down there . . . man, dig the redwood country way back in . . . reminds me of old Colorady b'god when I used to steal a car every day and drive out to hills like this with a fresh little high school sumptin"—"Yum Yum," says Dave Wain emphatically turning that big goofy look to us from his driving wheel with his big mad feverish shining eyes full of yumyum and yabyum too—"S'matter with you boys not making extensive plans to bring a bevy of schoolgirls down here to wile away our conversation pieces thar" says Cody real relaxed and talking sadly.

Behind us the Monsanto jeepster follows doggedly—Passing thru Monterey Monsanto has already called Pat McLear, staying for the summer with wife and kid in Santa Cruz, McLear with his own jeepster is following us a few miles down the highway—It's a big Big Sur day.

We wheel downhill to cross the creek and at the corral fence I proudly get out to officially open the gate and let the cars through—We go bumping down the two-rutted lane to the cabin and park—My heart sinks to see the cabin.

To see the cabin so sad and almost human waiting there for me as if forever, to hear my little neat gurgling creek resuming its song just for me, to see the very same bluejays still waiting in the tree for me and maybe mad at me now they see I'm back because I havent been there to lay out their Cheerios along the porch rail every blessed morning—And in fact first thing I do is rush inside and get them some food and lay it out—But so many people around now they're afraid to try it.

Monsanto all decked out in his old clothes and looking forward to a wine and talkfest weekend in his pleasant cabin takes the big sweet axe down from the wall nails and goes out and starts hammering at a huge log—In fact it's really a half of a tree that fell there years ago and's been hammered at intermittently but now he's bound he's going to crack it in half and again in half so we can then start splitting it down the middle for huge bonfire type logs—Meanwhile little Arthur Ma who never goes anywhere without his drawing paper and his Yellowjack felt tip pencils is already seated in my chair on the porch (wearing my hat now too) drawing one of his interminable pictures, he'll do 25 a day and 25 the next day too—He'll talk and go on drawing—He has felt tips of all colors, red, blue, yellow, green, black, he draws marvelous subconscious glurbs and can also do excellent objective scenes or anything he wants on to cartoons—Dave is taking my rucksack and his rucksack out of Willie and throwing them into the cabin, Ben Fagan is wandering around near the creek puffing on his pipe with a happy bhikku smile, Ron Blake is unpacking the steaks we bought enroute in Monterey and I'm already flicking the plastics off the top of bottles with that expert twitch and twist you only get to learn after years of winoing in alleys east and west.

Still the same, the fog is blowing over the walls of the canyon obscuring the sun but the sun keeps fighting back—The inside of the cabin with the fire finally going is still the dear lovable abode now as sharp in my mind as I look at it as an unusually well focused snapshot—The sprig of ferns still stands in a glass of water, the books are there, the neat groceries ranged along the wall shelves—I feel excited to be with the gang but there's a hidden sadness too and which is expressed later by Monsanto when he says "This is the kind of place where a person should really be alone, you know? when you bring a big gang here it somehow desecrates it not that I'm referring to us or anybody in particular? there's such a sad sweetness to those trees as tho yells shouldnt insult them or conversation only"—Which is just the way I feel too.

In a gang we all go down the path towards the sea, passing underneath "That *sonof*abitch bridge" Cody calls it looking up with horror—"That thing's enough to scare anybody away"—But worst of all for an old driver like Cody, and Dave too, is to see that upended old chassis in the sand, they spend a half hour poking around the wreckage and shaking their heads—We kick around the beach awhile and decide to come back at night with bottles and flashlights and build a huge bonfire, now it's time to get back to the cabin and cook those steaks and have a ball, and there's McLear's jeep already arrived and parked and there's McLear himself and that beautiful blonde wife of his in her tight blue jeans that makes Dave say "Yum yum" and Cody just say "Yes, that's right, yes, that's right, ah hum honey, yes."

19

A ROARING DRINKING BOUT begins deep in the canyon—Fog nightfall
sends cold seeping into the windows so all these softies demand that
the wood windows be closed so we all sit there in the glow of the one
lamp coughing in the smoke but they dont care—They think it's just
the steaks smoking over the fire—I have one of the jugs in my hand
and I wont let go—McLear is the handsome young poet who's just
written the most fantastic poem in America, called "Dark Brown,"
which is every detail of his and his wife's body described in ecstatic
union and communion and inside out and everywhichaway and not
only that he insists on reading it to us—But I wanta read my "Sea"
poem too—But Cody and Dave Wain are talking about something
else and that silly kid Ron Blake is singing like Chet Baker—Arthur
Ma is drawing in the corner, and it sorta goes like this generally:—
   "That's what old men do, Cody, they drive slowly backwards in
Safeway Supermarket parking lots"—"Yes that's right, I was tellin
you about that bicycle of mine but that's what they do yes you see
that's because while the old woman is shoppin in that store they figure
they'll park a little closer to the entrance and so they spend a half
hour to think their big move out and they back in out slowly from
their slot, can hardly turn around to see what's in back, usually nothin
there, then they wheel real slow and trembly to that slot they picked
but all of a sudden some cat jumps in it with his pickup and them old
men is scratchin their heads sayin and whining 'Owww, these young
fellers nowadays' and all that obvious, ah, yes, but that BICYCLE
of mine in Denver I tell you I had it twisted and that wheel used to
wobble so by necissity I had to invent a new way to maneuver them
handlebars see—"—"Hey Cody have a drink," I'm yelling in his ear
and meanwhile McLear is reading: "Kiss my thighs in darkness the
pit of fire" and Monsanto is chuckling saying to Fagan: "So this crazy
character comes down stairs and asking for a copy of Alisteir Crowley

and I didnt know 'bout that till you told me the other day, then on the way out I see him sneak a book off the shelf but he puts another one in its place that he got out of his pocket, and the books is a novel by somebody called Denton Welch all about this young kid in China wanderin around the streets like real romantic young Truman Capote only it's China" and Arthur Ma suddenly yells: "Hold still you buncha bastards, I got a hole in my eye" and generally the way parties go, and so on, ending with the steak dinner (I dont even touch a bite but just drink on), then the big bonfire on the beach to which we march all in one arm-swinging gang, I've gotten the idea in my head I'm the leader of a guerilla warfare unit and I'm marching ahead the lieutenant giving orders, with all our flashlights and yells we come swarming down the narrow path going "Hup one two three" and challenging the enemy to come out of hiding, some guerillas.

Monsanto that old woodsman starts a huge bonfire on the beach that can be seen flaring from miles away, cars passing across the bridge way up there can see there's a party goin on in the hole of night, in fact the bonfire lights up the eerie weird beams and staunches of the bridge almost all the way up, giant shadows dance on the rocks— The sea swirls up but seems subdued—It's not like being alone down in the vast hell writing the sounds of the sea.

The night ending with everybody passing out exhausted on cots, in sleepingbags outside (McLear goes home with wife) but Arthur Ma and I by the late fire keep up yelling spontaneous questions and answers right till dawn like "Who told you you had a hat on your head?"—"My head never questions hats"—"What's the matter with your liver training?"—"My liver training got involved in kidney work"—(and here again another great gigantic little Oriental friend for me, an eastcoaster who's never known Chinese or Japanese kids, on the west coast it's quite common but for an eastcoaster like me it's amazing and what with all my earlier studies in Zen and Chan and Tao)—(And Arthur also being a gentle small softhaired seemingly soft little Oriental goofnik)—And we come to great chanted statements, taking turns, without a pause to think, just one then the other, bing and bang, the beauty of them being that while one guy is yelling like (me):- "Tonight the full apogee August moon will out, early with

a jaundiced tint, and pop angels all over my rooftop along with Devas
sprinkling flowers" (any kind of nonsense being the rule) the other
guy has time not only to figure the next statement but can take off
from the subconscious arousement of an idea from "angels all over
my rooftop" and so can yell without thinking an answer the stupider
or rather the more unexpectedly insaner sillier brighter it is the better
"Pilgrims dropping turds and sweet nemacular nameless railroad
trains from heaven with omnipotent youths bearing monkey women
that will stomp through the stage waiting for the moment when by
pinching myself I prove that a thought is like a touch"—But this is
only the beginning because now we know the routine and get better
and better till at dawn I seem to recall we were so fantastically bril-
liant (while everyone snored) the skies must have shook to hear it and
not just foil: let's see if I can recreate at least the style of this game:-

ARTHUR: "When are you going to become the Eighth Patriarch?"

ME: "As soon as you give me that old motheaten sweater"—(Much
better than that, forget this for now, because I want to talk first about
Arthur Ma and try again to duplicate our feat).

20

AS I SAY MY FIRST little Chinese friend, I keep saying "little" George and "little" Arthur but the fact is they were both small anyway— Altho George talked slowly and was a little absent from everything in the way of a Zen Master actually who realizes that everything is indifferent anyway, Arthur was friendlier, warmer in a way, curious and always asking questions, more active than George with his constant drawing, and of course Chinese instead of Japanese—He wanted me to meet his father the following weeks—He was Monsanto's best friend at the time and they made an extremely strange pair going down the street together, the big ruddy happy man with the crew-cut and corduroy jacket and sometimes pipe in mouth, and the little childlike Chinese boy who looked so young most bartenders wouldnt serve him tho he was actually 30 years old—Nevertheless the son of a famous Chinatown family and Chinatown is right back there behind the fabled beatnik streets of Frisco—Also Arthur was a tremendous little loverboy who had fabulously beautiful girls on the line and however'd just separated from his wife, a girl I never saw but Monsanto told me she was the most beautiful Negro girl in the world—Arthur came from a large family but as a painter and a Bohemian his family disapproved of him now so he lived alone in a comfortable old hotel on North Beach tho sometimes he went around the corner into Chinatown to visit his father who sat in the back of his Chinese general store brooding among his countless poems written swiftly in Chinese stroke on pieces of beautiful colored paper which he then hanged from the ceiling of his little cubicle—There he sat, clean, neat, almost shiney, wondering about what poem to write next but his keen little eyes always jumping to the street door to see who's going by and if someone came into the shop itself he knew at once who it was and for what—He was in fact the best friend and trusted adviser of Chiang Kai Shek in America, true and no lie—But Arthur himself was in

favor of the Red Chinese which was a family matter and a Chinese
matter I had nothing to say about and didnt interest me except insofar
as it gave a dramatic picture of father and son in an old culture—The
point of the matter anyway being that he was goofing with me just like
George had done and making me happy somehow like George had
done—Something anciently familiar about his loyal presence made
me wonder if I'd ever lived before in some other lifetime in China or
if he'd been an Occidental himself in a previous lifetime of his own
involved with mine somewhere else than China—The pity of it is that
I have no record of what we were yelling and announcing back and
forth as the birds woke up outside but it went generally like this:-

ME:- "Unless someone sicks a hot iron in my heart or heaps up Evil
Karma like tit and tat the pile of that and pulls my mother out her bed
to slay her before my damning human eyes—"

ARTHUR:- "And I break my hand on heads—"

ME:- "Everytime you throw a rock at a cat from your glass house
you heap upon yourself the automatic Stanley Gould winter so dark of
death after death, and growing old—"

ARTHUR:- "Because lady those ashcans'll bite you back and be cold
too—"

ME:- "And your son will never rest in the imperturbable knowledge
that what he thinks he thinks as well as what he does he thinks as well
as what he feels he thinks as well as future that—"

ARTHUR:- "Future that my damn old sword cutter Paisan Pasha
lost the Preakness again—"

ME:- "Tonight the moon shall witness angels trooping at the baby's
window where inside he gurgles in his pewk looking with mewling
eyes for babyside waterfall lambikin hillside the day the little Arab
shepherd boy hugged the babylamb to heart while the mother bleeted
at his bay heel—"

ARTHUR:- "And so Joe the sillicks killit no not—"

ME:- "Shhhhoww graaa—"

ARTHUR:- "Wind and carstart—"

ME:- "The angels Devas monsters Asuras Devadattas Vedantas
McLaughlins Stones will hue and hurl in hell if they dont love the
lamb the lamb the lamb of hell lamb-chop—"

ARTHUR:- "Why did Scott Fitzgerald keep a notebook?"

ME:- "Such a marvelous notebook—"

ARTHUR:- "Komi denera ness pata sutyamp anda wanda vesnoki shadakiroo paryoumemga sikarem nora sarkadium baron roy kellegiam myorki ayastuna haidanseetzel ampho andiam yerka yama chelmsford alya bonneavance koroom cemanda versel—"

ME:- "The 26th Annual concert of the Armenian Convention?"

21

INCIDENTALLY I FORGOT TO MENTION that during the three weeks alone the stars had not come out at all, not even for one minute on any night, it was the foggy season, except the very last night when I was getting ready to leave—Now the stars were out every night, the sun shone considerably longer but a sinister wind accompanied the Autumn in Big Sur: it seemed like the whole Pacific Ocean was blowing with all its might right into Raton Canyon and also over the high gap from another end causing all the trees to shudder as the big groaning howl came newsing and noising from downcanyon, when it hit there was raised a roar of noise I didnt like—It seemed ill omened to me somewhere—It was much better to have fog and silence and quiet trees—Now the whole canyon by one blast could be led screaming and waving in all directions in such a confused mass that even the fellows with me were a little surprised to see it—It was too big a wind for such a little canyon.

This development also prevented the constant hearing of the reassuring creek.

One good thing was that when jet planes broke the sound barrier overhead the wind dispersed the clap of empty thunder they caused, because during the foggy season the noise would come down into the canyon, concentrate there, and rock the house like an explosion making me think the first time (alone) that somebody'd set off a blast of dynamite nearby.

While I woke up groaning and sick there was plenty of wine right there to start me off with the hounds of hair, so okay, but Monsanto had retired early and typically sensibly to sleep by the creek and now he was awake singing swooshing his whole head into the creek and going Brrrrr and rubbing his hands for a new day—Dave Wain made breakfast with his usual lecture "Now the real way to fry eggs is to put a cover over them so that they can have that neat basted white look on the yellows, soon's I get this pancake batter ready we'll start on them"—My list of groceries was so all inclusive in the beginning it was now feeding guerilla troops.

A big axe chopping contest began after breakfast, some of us sitting watching on the porch and the performers down below hacking away at the tree trunk which was over a foot thick—They were chopping off two foot chunks, no easy job—I realized you can always study the character of a man by the way he chops wood—Monsanto an old lumberman up in Maine as I say now showed us how he conducted his whole life in fact by the way he took neat little short handled chops from both left and right angles getting his work done in reasonably short time without too much sweat—But his strokes were rapid—Whereas old Fagan pipe-in-mouth slogged away I guess the way he learned in Oregon and in the Northwest fire schools, also getting his job done, silently, not a word—But Cody's fantastic fiery character showed in the way he went at the log with horrible force, when he brought down the axe with all his might and holding it far at the end you could hear the whole tree-trunk groaning the whole length inside, runk, sometimes you could hear a lengthwise cracking going on, he is really very strong and he brought that axe down so hard his feet left the earth when it hit—He chopped off his log with the fury of a Greek god—Nevertheless it took him longer and much more sweat than Monsanto—"Used to do this in a workgang in southern Arizony" he said, whopping one down that made the whole treetrunk dance off the ground—But it was like an example of vast but senseless strength, a picture of poor Cody's life and in a sense my own—I too chopped with all my might and got madder and went faster and raked the log but took more time than Monsanto who watched us smiling—Little Arthur thereupon tried his luck but gave up after five strokes—The axe was like to carry him away anyway—Then Dave Wain demonstrated with big easy strokes and in no time we had five huge logs to use—But now it was time to get in the cars (McLear had rearrived) and go driving south down the coast highway to a hot springs bath house down there, which sounded good to me at first.

But the new Big Sun Autumn was now all winey sparkling blue which made the terribleness and giantness of the coast all the more

clear to see in all its gruesome splendor, miles and miles of it snak-
ing away south, our three jeeps twisting and turning the increasing
curves, sheer drops at our sides, further ghostly high bridges to cross
with smashings below—Tho all the boys are wowing to see it—To me
it's just an inhospitable madhouse of the earth, I've seen it enough and
even swallowed it in that deep breath—The boys reassure me the hot
springs bath will do me good (they see I'm gloomy now hungover for
good) but when we arrive my heart sinks again as McLear points out
to sea from the balcony of the outdoor pools: "Look out there floating
in the sea weeds, a dead otter!"—And sure enough it is a dead otter I
guess, a big brown pale lump floating up and down mournfully with
the swells and ghastly weeds, my otter, my dear otter I'd written poems
about—"Why did he die?" I ask myself in despair—"Why do they do
that?"—"What's the sense of all this?"—All the fellows are shading
their eyes to get a better look at the big peaceful tortured hunk of
seacow out there as tho it's something of passing interest while to me
it's a blow across the eyes and down into my heart—The hot water
pools are steaming, Fagan and Monsanto and the others are all sitting peacefully up to their necks, they're all naked, but there's a gang
of fairies also there naked all standing around in various bath house
postures that make me hesitate to take my clothes off just on general
principles—In fact Cody doesnt even bother to do anything but lie
down with his clothes on in the sun, on the balcony table, and just
smoke—But I borrow McLear's yellow bathingsuit and get in—"What
ya wearing a bathingsuit in a hot springs pool for boy?" says Fagan
chuckling—With horror I realize there's spermatazoa floating in the
hot water—I look and I see the other men (the fairies) all taking good
long looks at Ron Baker who stands there facing the sea with his arse
for all to behold, not to mention McLear and Dave Wain too—But it's
very typical of me and Cody that we wont undress in this situation
(we were both raised Catholics?)—Supposedly the big sex heroes of
our generation, in fact—You might think—But the combination of
the strange silent watching fairy-men, and the dead otter out there,
and the spermatazoa in the pools makes me sick, not to mention that
when somebody informs me this bath house is owned by the young
writer Kevin Cudahy whom I knew very well in New York and I ask

one of the younger strangers where's Kevin Cudahy he doesnt even
deign to reply—Thinking he hasnt heard me I ask again, no reply, no
notice, I ask a third time, this time he gets up and stalks out angrily to
the locker rooms—It all adds up to the confusion that's beginning to
pile up in my battered drinking brain anyway, the constant reminders
of death not the least of which was the death of my peaceful love of
Raton Canyon now suddenly becoming a horror.

From the baths we go to Nepenthe which is a beautiful cliff top
restaurant with vast outdoor patio, with excellent food, excellent
waiters and management, good drinks, chess tables, chairs and tables
to just sit in the sun and look at the grand coast—Here we all sit at
various tables and Cody starts playing chess with everybody will
join while he's chomping away at those marvelous hamburgers called
Heavenburgers (huge with all the side works)—Cody doesnt like
to just sit around and lightly chat away, he's the kind of guy if he's
going to talk he has to do all the talking himself for hours till everything is exhaustedly explained, sans that he just wants to bend over a
chessboard and say "He he heh, old Scrooge is saving up a pawn hey?
cak! I got ya!"—But while I'm sitting there discussing literature with
McLear and Monsanto suddenly a strange couple of gentlemen nearby
strike up an acquaintance—One of them is a youngster who says he
is a lieutenant in the Army—I instantly (drunk on fifth Manhattan by
now) go into my theory of guerilla warfare based on my observations
the night before when it did seriously occur to me that if Monsanto,
Arthur, Cody, Dave, Ben, Ron Blake and I were all members of one
fighting unit (and all carrying canteens of booze on our belts) it would
be very difficult for the enemy to hurt any of us because we'd be, as
dear friends, watching so desperately closely over one another, which
I tell the first lieutenant, which attracts the interest of the older man
who admits that he's a GENERAL in the Army—There are also some
further homosexuals at a separate table which prompts Dave Wain to
look up from the chess game at one quiet drowsy point and announce
in his dry twang "Under redwood beams, people talking about homo-
sexuality and war . . . call it my Nepenthe Haiku"—"Yass" says Cody
checkmating him "see what you can *ku* about that m'boy and get out
of there and I'll noose you with my queen, dear."

I mention the general only because there are also something sinister about the fact that during this long binge I came across him and *another* general, two strange generals, and I'd never met any generals in my life—This first general was strange because he seemed too polite and yet there was something sinister about his steely eyes behind goof darkglasses—Something sinister too about the first lieutenant who guessed who we were (the San Francisco poets, a major nucleus of them indeed) and didn't seem at all pleased tho the general seemed amused—Nevertheless in a sinister way the general seemed to take great interest in my theory about buddy units for guerilla warfare and when President Kennedy about a year later ordered just such a new scheme for part of our armed forces I wondered (still crazy even then but for new reasons) if the general had got an idea from me—The second general, even stranger, coming up, occurred when I was even more far gone.

Manhattans and more Manhattans and finally when we got back to the cabin in late afternoon I was feeling good but realized I was going to be finished tomorrow—But poor young Ron Blake asked me if he could stay with me in the cabin, the others were all going back to the city in the three cars, I couldnt think of any way to reject his request in a harmless way so said yes—So when they all left suddenly I was alone with this mad beatnik kid singing me songs and all I wanta do is sleep—But I've got to make the best of it and not disappoint his believing heart.

Because after all the poor kid actually believes that there's something noble and idealistic and kind about all this beat stuff, and I'm supposed to be the King of the Beatniks according to the newspapers, so but at the same time I'm sick and tired of all the endless enthusiasms of new young kids trying to know me and pour out all their lives into me so that I'll jump up and down and say yes yes that's right, which I cant do any more—My reason for coming to Big Sur for the summer being precisely to get away from that sort of thing— Like those pathetic five highschool kids who all came to my door in Long Island one night wearing jackets that said "Dharma Bums" on them, all expecting me to be 25 years old according to a mistake on a book jacket and here I am old enough to be their father—But no, hep swinging young jazzy Ron wants to dig everything, go to the beach, run and romp and sing, talk, write tunes, write stories, climb mountains, go hiking, see everything, do everything with everybody—But having one last quart of port with me I agree to follow him to the beach.

We go down the old sad path of the bhikku and suddenly I see a dead mouse in the grass—"A wee dead mousie" I say cleverly poetically but suddenly I realize and remember now for the first time how I've left the cover off the rat poison in Monsanto's shelf and so this is *my mouse*—It's lying there *dead*—Like the otter in the sea—It's my own personal mouse that I've carefully fed chocolate and cheese all summer but once again I've unconsciously sabotaged all these great plans of mine to be kind to living beings even bugs, once again I've murdered a mouse one way or the other—And on top of that when we come to the place where the garter snake usually lies sunning itself, and I bring it to Ron's attention, he suddenly yells "LOOKOUT! you never can tell what kind of snake it is!" which really scares me, my heart pounds with horror—My little friend the garter snake turns therefore with my head from a living being with a long green body into the evil serpent of Big Sur.

On top of that, at the surf, where long streamers of hollow sea weed always lie around drying in the sun some of them huge, like living bodies with skin, pieces of living material that always made me sad somehow, here's the young hepcat lifting them up and dancing a dervish around the beach with them, turning my Sur into something seachange—Something brainchange.

All that night by lamplight we sing and yell songs which is okay but in the morning the bottle is gone and I wake up with the "final horrors" again, precisely the way I woke up in the Frisco skidrow room before escaping down here, it's all caught up with me again, I can hear myself again whining "Why does God torture me?"—But anybody who's never had delirium tremens even in their early stages may not understand that it's not so much a physical pain but a mental anguish indescribable to those ignorant people who dont drink and accuse drinkers of irresponsibility—The mental anguish is so intense that you feel you have betrayed your very birth, the efforts nay the birth pangs of your mother when she bore you and delivered you to the world, you've betrayed every effort your father ever made to feed you and raise you and make you strong and my God even educate you for "life," you feel a guilt so deep you identify yourself with the devil and God seems far away abandoning you to your sick silliness—You feel sick in the greatest sense of the word, *breathing without believing in it,* sicksicksick, your soul groans, you look at your helpless hands as tho they were on fire and you cant move to help, you look at the world with dead eyes, there's on your face an expression of incalculable repining like a constipated angel on a cloud—In fact it's actually a cancerous look you throw on the world, through browngray wool fuds over your eyes—Your tongue is white and disgusting, your teeth are stained, your hair seems to have dried out overnight, there are huge mucks in the corners of your eyes, greases on your nose, froth at the sides of your mouth: in short that very disgusting and wellknown hideousness everybody knows who's walked past a city street drunk in the Boweries of the world—But there's no joy at all, people say "Oh well he's drunk and happy let him sleep it off"—The poor drunkard is *crying*—He's crying for his mother and father and great brother and great friend, he's crying for help—He tries to pull himself together by moving one shoe nearer to his foot and he cant even do that properly, he'll drop the shoe, or knock something over, he'll do something invariably that'll start him crying again—He'll want to bury his face in his hands and moan for mercy and he knows there is none—Not only because he doesnt deserve it but there's no such thing anyway—Because he looks up at the blue sky and there's nothing there but empty space making a big face at him—He looks at the world, it's sticking its tongue out at him and once that mask is removed it's looking at him with hollow big red eyes like his own eyes—He may see the earth move but there's no significance of any particular kind to attach to that—One little unexpected noise behind him will make him snarl in rage—He'll pull and tug at his poor stained shirt—He feels like rubbing his face into something that isnt.

His socks are thick tired moisty slimes—The beard on his cheeks itches the running sweats and annoys the tortured mouth—There's a twisted feeling of no-more, never-again, agh—What was beautiful and clean yesterday has irrationally and unaccountably changed into a big dreary crock of shit—The hairs on his fingers stare at him like tomb hairs—The shirt and trousers have become glued to his person as tho he was to be drunk forever—The ache of remorse sinks in as tho somebody was pushing it in from above—The pretty white clouds in the sky hurt his eyes only—The only thing to do is turn over and lie face down and weep—The mouth is so blasted there's not even a chance to gnash the teeth—There's not even strength to tear the hair.

And here comes Ron Blake starting off his new day singing at the top of his voice—I go down by the creek and throw myself in the sand and lie looking with sad eyes at the water which no longer friends me but sorta wants me to go away—There isnt a drop to drink left in the cabin, all the goddamn jeeps are gone with all its healthy cargo of people and I'm alone with an enthusiastic kid on a lark—The little bugs I'd saved from drowning just because I was bemused and alone and glad, now drown unnoticed within my reach anyway—The spider is still minding his own business in the outhouse—Alf lows mournfully in the valley far away to express just the way I feel—The bluejays yak around me as tho because I'm too tired and helpless to feed them any more they're figuring on trying me if they can, "They're friggin vultures anyway" I moan with my mouth in the sand—The once pleasant thumpthump gurgle slap of the creek is now an endless jabbering of blind nature which doesnt understand anything in the first place—My old thoughts about the slit of a billion years covering all this and all cities and generations eventually is just a dumb old thought, "Only a silly sober fool could think it, imagine gloating over such nonsense" (because in one sense the drinker learns wisdom, in the words of Goethe or Blake or whichever it was "The pathway to wisdom lies through excess")—But in this condition you can only say "Wisdom is just another way to make people sick"—"I'm SICK" I yell emphatically to the trees, to the woods around, to the hills above, looking around desperately, nobody cares—I can even hear Ron singing at his lunch inside.

What's even more horrible he tries to show compunction and wants to help me, "Anything I can do"—Later he goes for a lone walk so I go in the cabin and lie on the cot and spend about two hours groaning out a lament: "*O mon Dieux, pourquoi Tu m'laisse faire malade comme ça—Papa Papa aide mué—Aw j'ai mal au coeur—J'envie d'aller à toilette 'pi ça m'interesse pas—Aw 'shu malade*—Owaowaowao—" (I go into a long "awaowaowoa" that I guess lasted a whole minute)—I toss over and find new reasons to groan—I think I'm alone and I'm letting it all go a whole lot like I'd heard my father do when he was dying of cancer in the night in the bed next to mine—When I do manage to stagger up and go lean on the door I realize with double upon double horror that Ron Blake has been sitting there all this time listening to everything over a book—(I wonder now what he told people about this later, it must have sounded horrible)—(Idiotic too, cretinous even, maybe only French Canadian who knows?)—"Ron I'm sorry you had to hear all that, I'm sick"—"I know, man, it's okay, lie down and try to sleep"—"I cant sleep!" I yell in a rage—I feel like yelling "Fuck yourself you little idiot what do you know what Im going through!" but then I realize how oldman disgusting and hopeless all that is, and here he is enjoying his big weekend with the big writer he was supposed to tell all his friends what a great swinging ball it was and what I did and said—But methinks and mayhap he took away a lesson in temperance, or a lesson in beatness really—Because the only time I've ever been sicker and madder was a week later when Dave and I came back with the two girls leading to the final horrible night.

22

BUT LOOK AT THIS: in the afternoon restless youngster Ron wants to go hitch hiking to Monterey of all things to go see McLear and I say "Okay go ahead"—"Aint you coming with me?" he asks surprised to see the champion on-the-roader wont even hitch hike any more, "No I'll stay here and get better—I gotta be alone," which is true, because as soon as he's gone and has yelled one final hoot from the canyon road directly above and gone on, and I've sat in the sun alone on the porch, fed my birds finally again, washed my socks and shirt and pants and hung them up to dry on bushes, slurped up tons of water kneeling at the creek race, stared silently at the trees, soon as the sun goes down I swear on my arm I'm as well as I ever was: just like that suddenly.

"Can it be that Ron and all these other guys, Dave and McLear or somebody, the other guys earlier are all a big bunch of witches out to make me go mad?" I seriously consider this—Remembering that childhood revery I always had, which I used to ponder seriously as I walked home from St. Joseph's Parochial School or sat in the parlor of my home, that everybody in the world is making fun of money me and I dont know it because everytime I turn around to see who's behind me they snap back into place with regular expressions, but soon's I look away again they dart up to my nape of neck and all whisper there giggling and plotting evil, silently, you cant hear them, and when I turn quickly to catch them they've already snapped back perfectly in place and are saying "Now the proper way to cook eggs is" or they're singing Chet Baker songs looking the other way or they're saying "Did I ever tell you about Jim that time?"—But my childhood revery also included the fact that everybody in the world was making this fun of me because they were all members of an eternal secret society or Heaven society that knew the secret of the world and were seriously fooling me so I'd wake up and see the light (i.e., become enlightened, in fact)—So that I, "Ti Jean," was the LAST Ti Jean left in the world,

the last poor holy fool, those people at my neck were the devils of the
earth among whom God had cast me, an angel baby, as tho I was the
last Jesus in fact! and all these people were waiting for me to realize
it and wake up and catch them peeking and we'd all laugh in Heaven
suddenly—But animals werent doing that behind my back, my cats
were always adornments licking their paws sadly, and Jesus, he was
a sad witness to this, somewhat like the animals—He wasnt peeking
down my neck—There lies the root of my belief in Jesus—So that
actually the only reality in the world was Jesus and the lambs (the
animals) and my brother Gerard who had instructed me—Meanwhile
some of the peekers were kindly and sad, like my father, but had to
go along with everybody else in the same boat—But my waking up
would take place and then everything would vanish except Heaven,
which is God—And that was why later in life after these rather strange
you must admit childhood reveries, after I had that fainting vision of
the Golden Eternity and others before and after it including Samadhis
during Buddhist meditations in the woods, I conceived of myself as
a special solitary angel sent down as a messenger from Heaven to tell
everybody or show everybody by example that their peeking society
was actually the Satanic Society and they were all on the wrong track.

With all this in my background, now at the point of adulthood
disaster of the soul, through excessive drinking, all this was easily
converted into a fantasy that everybody in the world was witching me
to madness: and I must have believed it subconsciously because as I
say as soon as Ron Blake left I was well again and in fact content.

In fact very contented—I rose that following morning with more
joy and health and purpose than ever, and there was me old Big Sur
Valley all mine again, here came good old Alf and I gave him food
and patted his big rough neck with its various cocotte's manes, there
was the mountain of Mien Mo in the distance just a dismal old hill
with funny bushes around the sides and a peaceful farm on top, and
nothing to do all day but amuse myself undisturbed by witches and
booze—And I'm singing ditties again "My soul aint snow, wouldnt
you know, the color of my soul, is interpole" and such silly stuff—And
I yell "If Arthur Ma is a witch he sure is a funny witch! har har!"—And
there's the bluejay idiot with one foot on the bar of soap on the porch

rail, pecking at the soap and eating it, leaving the cereal unattended, and when I laugh and yell at him he looks up cute with an expression that seems to say "What's the matter? wotti do wong?"—"Wo wo, got the wong place," said another bluejay landing nearby and suddenly leaving again—And everything of my life seems beautiful again, I even start remembering the nutty things of the binge and go back even farther and remember nutty things all through my life, it's just amazing how inside our own souls we can lift out so much strength I think it would be enough strength to move mountains at that, to lift our boots up again and go clomping along happy out of nothing but the good source power in our own bones—And when I visit the sea it doesnt scare me anymore, I just sing out "Seventy thousand schemers in the sea" and go back to my cabin and just quietly pour my coffee in the cup, afternoon, how pleasant!

I make a wood run, axe and yank logs outa everywhichawhere and leave em by the side of the road to leisurely carry home—I investigate a cabin down the creek that has 15 wood matches in it for my emergency—Take a shot of sherry, hate it—Find an old San Francis Chronicle with my name in it all over—Hack a giant redwood log in half in the middle of the creek—That kind of day, perfect, ending up sewing my holy sweater singing "There's no place like home" remembering my mother—I even plunge into all the books and magazines around, I read up on 'Pataphysics and yell contemptuously in the lamplight "'T'sa'n intellectual excuse for facetious joking," throwing the magazine away, adding "Peculiarly attractive to certain shallow types"—Then I turn my rumbling attention to a couple of unknown *Fin du Siècle* poets called Theo Marzials and Henry Harland—I take a nap after supper and dream of the U.S. Navy, a ship anchored near a war scene, at an island, but everything is drowsy as two sailors go up the trail with fishingpoles and a dog between them to go make love quietly in the hills: the captain and everybody know they're queer and rather than being infuriated however they're all drowsily enchanted by such gentle love: you see a sailor peeking after them with binoculars from the poop: there's supposed to be a war but nothing happens, just laundry. . .

I wake up from this silly but strangely pretty dream feeling exhilirated—Besides now the stars come out every night and I go out on that porch and sit in the old canvas chair and turn my face up to all that mooching going on up there, starmooched firmament, all those stars crying with happy sadness, all that ream and cream of mocky ways with alleyways of lightyears old as Dame Mae Whitty and the hills—I go walking towards Mien Mo mountain in the moon illuminated August night, see gorgeous misty mountains rising the horizon and like saying to me "You dont have to torture your consciousness with endless thinking" so I sit in the sand and look inward and see those old roses of the unborn again—Amazing, and in just a few hours this change—And I have enough physical energy to walk back to the sea suddenly realizing what a beautiful oriental silk scroll painting this whole canyon would make, those scrolls you open slowly at one end and keep unrolling and unrolling as the valley unfolds towards sudden cliffs, sudden Bodhisattvas sitting alone in lamplit huts, sudden creeks, rocks, trees, then sudden white sand, sudden sea, out to sea and you've reached the end of the scroll—And with all those misty rose darknesses of varying tint and tuckaway shades to express the actual ephemerality of night—One long roll unfurling from the range fence among the misty hills, moon meadows, even the hay rick near the creek, down to the trail, the narrowing creek, then the mystery of the AW SEA—So I investigate the scroll of the valley but I'm singing "Man is a busy little animal, a nice little animal, his thoughts about everything, dont amount to shit."

In fact back at the cabin to make my bedtime hot Ovaltine I even sing "Sweet Sixteen" like an angel (by God bettern Ron Blake) and all the old memories of Ma and Pa, the upright piano in old Massachusetts, the old summernight sings—That's how I go to sleep, under the stars on the porch, and at dawn I turn over with a blissful smile on my face because the owls are callin and answering from two different huge dead trunks across the valley, hoo hoo hoo.

So maybe it's true what Milarepa says: "Though you youngsters of the new generation dwell in towns infested with deceitful fate, the link of truth still remains"—(and said this in 890!)—"When you remain in solitude, do not think of the amusements in the town. . . You should turn your mind inwardly, and then you'll find your way. . .

The wealth I found is the inexhaustible Holy Property. . . The companion I found is the bliss of perpetual Voidness. . . Here in the place of Yolmo Tag Pug Senge Dzon, the tigress howling with a pathetic trembling voice reminds me that her piteous cubs are playing lively. . . Like a madman I have no pretension and no hope. . . I am telling you the honest truth. . . These are the crazy words of mine. . . O h you innumerable motherlike beings, by the force of imaginary destiny you see a myriad visions and experience endless emotions. . . I smile. . . To a Yogi, everything is fine and splendid!. . . . . In the goodly quiet of this Self-Benefitting sky Enclosure, the timely sounds I hear are all my fellows' sounds. . . At such a pleasant place, in solitude, I, Milarepa, happily remain, meditating upon the void-illuminating mind—The more Ups and Downs the more Joy I feel—The greater the fear, the greater the happiness I feel. . ."

23

BUT IN THE MORNING (and I'm no Milarepa who could also sit naked in the snow and was seen flying on one occasion) here comes Ron Blake back with Pat McLear and Pat's wife the beautiful one, and by God their little sweet 5 year old girl who is such a pleasant sight to see as she goes jongling and jiggling through the fields to look for flowers, everything to her is perfectly new beautiful primordial Garden of Eden morning here in this tortured human canyon—And a rather beautiful morning develops—There's fog so we close the blinds and light the fire and the lamp, me and Pat, and sit there drinking from the jug he brought talking about literature and poetry while his wife listens and occasionally gets up to heat more coffee and tea or goes out to play with Ron and the little girl—Pat and I are in a serious talkative mood and I feel that lonely shiver in my chest which always warns me: you actually love people and you're glad Pat is here.

Pat is one if not THE most handsome man I've ever seen—Strange that he's announced in a preface to his poems that his heroes, his Triumvirate, are Jean Harlow, Rimbaud and Billy the Kid because he himself is handsome enough to play Billy the Kid in the movies, that same darkhaired handsome slightly sliteyed look you expect from the myth appearance of Billy the Kid (I suppose not the actual real life William Bonnie who's said to've been a pimply cretin monster).

So we launch on a big discussion of everything in the comfortable gloom of the cabin by the warm red glow of the girly fire, I'm wearing dark glasses anyway for fun, Pat says "Well Jack I didnt have a chance to talk to you yesterday or even last year or even ten years ago when I first met you, I remember I was terrified of you and Pomeray when you ran up my steps one night with sticks of tea, you looked like a couple of car thieves or bank robbers—And you know a lot of this sneery stuff they've written against us, against San Francisco or beat poetry and writers is because a lot of us dont LOOK like writers

or intellecuals or anything, you and Pomeray I must say look awful
in a way, I'm sure I dont fill the bill either"—"Man you oughta go to
Hollywood and play Billy the Kid"—"Man I'd rather go to Hollywood
and play Rimbaud"—"Well you cant play Jean Harlow"—"I'd really
like to just get my 'Dark Brown' published in Paris, do you know that
when you think it's possible a word from you to Gallimard or Girodias
would help"—"I dunno"—"Do you know that when I read your poems
Mexico City Blues I immediately turned around and started writing a
brand new way, you enlightened me with that book"—"But it's nothing like what you do, in fact it's miles away, I am a language spinner
and you're idea man" and so on we talk till about noon and Ron's been
in and out, 's'made jaunts to the beach with the little ladies and Pat
and I dont realize the sun has come out but still sit there deep in the
cabin by now talking about Villon and Cervantes.

Suddenly, boom, the door of the cabin is flung open with a loud
crash and a burst of sunlight illuminates the room and I see an Angel
standing arm outstretched in the door!—It's Cody! all dressed in his
Sunday best in a suit! beside him are ranged several graduating golden
angels from Evelyn golden beautiful wife down to the most dazzling
angel of them all little Timmy with the sun striking off his hair in
beams!—It's such an incredible sight and surprise that both Pat and
I rise from our chairs involuntarily, like we've been lifted up in awe,
or scared, tho I dont feel scared so much as ecstatically amazed as tho
I've seen a vision—And the way Cody stands there not saying a word
with his arm outstretched for some reason, struck a pose of some sort
to surprise us or warn us, he's so much like St. Michael at the moment
it's unbelievable especially as I also suddenly realize what he's just
actually done, he's had wife and kiddies sneak up ever so quiet up the
porch steps (which are noisy and creaky), across the wood planks,
easy and tiptoeing, stood there awhile while he prepared to fling the
door open, all lined up and stood straight, then pow, he's opened the
door and thrown the golden universe into the dazzled mystic eyes of
big hip Pat McLcar and big amazed grateful me—It reminds me of
the time I once saw a whole tiptoeing gang of couples sneaking into
our back kitchen door on West Street in Lowell the leader telling me
to shush as I stand there 9 years old amazed, then all bursting in on

my father innocently listening to the Primo Carnera-Ernie Schaaft fight on the old 1930's radio—For a big roaring toot—But Cody's old-fashioned family tiptoe sneak carries that strange apocalyptic burst of gold he somehow always manages to produce, like I said elsewhere the time in Mexico he drove an old car over a rutted road very slowly as we were all high on tea and I saw golden Heaven, or the other times he's always seemed so golden like as I say in a davenport of some sort in Heaven in the golden top of Heaven.

Not that he means to produce this effect: he's just standing there with innate dramatic mystery holding forth his arm as if to say Behold, the sun! and Behold, the angels! sorta pointing at all the golden heads of his family and Pat and I stand aghast.

"Happy birthday Jack!" yells Cody or some such ordinary crazy inane greeting "I've come to you with good news! I've brought Evelyn and Emily and Gaby and Timmy because we're all so grateful and glad because everything has worked out absolutely dead perfect, or living perfect, boy, with that little old hunnerd dollars you gave me let me tell you the fantastic story of what happened" (to him it was utterly fantastic), "I went out and traded in my Nash that as you know wont even start but I have to have m'old buddies push it down the road for me, this guy had a perfect gem of a purple or what color is it Maw? magenty, slamelty, a *jeepster* station-wagon Jack but a perfect beauty mind you listen with a beautiful radio, a brand new set of backup lights, thisa and thata down to the perfect new tires and that wonderful shiney paint job, that color'll knock you out, that's what it is, Grape!" (as Evelyn murmurs the color) "Grape color for all the old grape wine jacks, so we've come here to not only thank you and see you again but to celebrate this, and on top of all that, occasion, goo me I'm all so gushy and girly, hee hee hee, yes that's right come on in children and then go out and get that gear in the car and get ready to sleep outdoors tonight and get that good open fresh air, Jack on top of all that and my heart is jess OVERflowin I got a NEW JOB!! along with that splissly little old beautiful new jeep! a new job right downtown in Los Gatos in fact I dont even have to drive to work any more, I can walk it, just half a mile, now Ma you come in here, meet old Pat McLear here, start up some eggs or some of that steak we brought,

open up that vieen roossee wine we brought for drunk old Jack that
good old boy while I personally private take him to walk with me back
down the road where the jeep is parked, unlock that gate, you got the
corral key Jack, okay, and we'll talk and walk just like old times and
drive back real slow in my new slowboat to China."

So it's a whole new day, a whole new situation the way it is with
Cody, in fact a whole new universe as suddenly we're alone again
really for the first time in ages walking rapidly down the road to go get
the car and he looks at me with that hand-rubbing wicked look like
he's about to spring a surprise on me that's the top surprise of them
all, "You guessed it old buddy I have here the LAST, the absolutely
LAST yet most perfect of all blackhaired seeded packed tight super-
bomber joints in the world which you and I are now going to light
up, 's'why I didnt want you to bring any of that wine right away, why
boy we got time to drink wine and wine and dance" and here he is
lighting up, says "Now dont walk too fast, it's time to stroll along like
we used to do remember sometimes on our daysoff on the railroad, or
walkin across that Third and Townsend tar like you said and the time
we watched the sun go down so perfect holy purple over that Mission
cross—Yessir, slow and easy, lookin at this gone valley" so we start
to puff the pot but as usual it creates doubtful paranoias in both our
minds and we actually sort of fall silent on the way to the car which is
a beautiful grape color at that, a brand new shiney Jeepster with all the
equipments, and the whole golden reunion deteriorates into Cody's
matter-of-fact lecture on why the car is going to be such a honey (the
technical details) and he even yells at me to hurry up with that corral
gate, "Cant wait here all day, hor hor hor."

But that's not the point, about pot paranoia, yet maybe it is at that—
I've long given it up because it bugs me anyway—But so we drive back
slowly to the shack and Evelyn and Pat's wife have met and are having
woman talk and McLear and I and Cody talk around the table planning excursions with the kids to the beach.

And there's Evelyn and I havent had a chance to talk to her for years
either, Oh the old days when we'd stay up late by the fireplace as I say
discussing Cody's soul, Cody this and Cody that, you could hear the
name Cody ringing under the roofs of America from coast to coast

almost to hear his women talking about him, always pronouncing "Cody" with a kind of anguish yet there was girlish squealing pleasure in it, "Cody has to learn to control the enormous forces in him" and Cody "will always modify his little white lies so much that they turn into black ones," and according to Irwin Garden Cody's women were always having transcontinental telephone talks about his dong (which is possible.)

Because he was always tremendously generated towards complete relationship with his women to the point where they ended up in one convoluted octopus mess of souls and tears and fellatio and hotel room schemes and rushing in and out of cars and doors and great crises in the middle of the night, wow that madman you can at least write on his grave someday "He Lived, He Sweated"—No halfway house is Cody's house—Tho now as I say sorta sweetly chastised and a little bored at last with the world after the crummy injustice of his arrest and sentence he's sorta quieted down and where he'd launch into a tremendous explanation of every one of his thoughts for the benefit of everybody in the room as he's putting on his socks and arranging his papers to leave, now he just flips it aside and may make a stale shrug—A Jesuit at work—Tho I remember one crazy moment in the shack that was typically Cody-like: complicated and simultane-ous with a million nuances as though the whole of creation suddenly exploded and imploded together in one moment: at the moment that Pat's pretty little angel daughter is coming in to hand me an extremely tiny flower ("It's for you," she says direct to me) (for some reason the poor little thing thinks I need a flower, or else her mother instructed her for charming reasons, like adornment) Cody is furiously explain-ing to his little son Tim "Never let the right hand know what your left hand is doing" and at that moment I'm trying to close my palm around the incredibly small flower and it's so small I cant even do that, cant feel it, cant hardly see it, in fact such a small flower only that little girl could have found it, but I look up to Cody as he says that to Tim, and also to impress Evelyn who's watching me, I announced "Never let the left hand know what the right hand is doing but this right hand cant even hold this flower" and Cody only looks up "Yass yass."

So what started as a big holy reunion and surprise party in Heaven deteriorates to a lot of showoff talk, actually, at least on my part, but when I get to drink the wine I feel lighter and we all go down to the beach—I walk in front with Evelyn but when we get to the narrow path I walk in front like an Indian to show her what a big Indian I've been all summer—I'm bursting to tell her everything—"See that grove there, once in a while you'll be surprised out of your shoes to see the mule quietly standing there with locks of hair like Ruth's over his forehead, a big Biblical mule meditating, or over there, but up here, and look at that bridge, now what do you think of that?"—All the kids are fascinated by the upsidedown car wreck—At one point I'm sitting in the sand as Cody walks up my way, I say to him him imitating Wallace Beery and scratching my armpits "Cuss a man for dyin in Death Valley" (the last lines of that great movie *Twenty Mule Team*) and Cody says "That's right, if anybody can imitate old Wallace Beery that's the only way to do it, you had just the right timber there in the tone of your voice there, *Cuss a man for dyin in Death Valley* hee hee yes" but he rushes off to talk to McLear's wife.

Strange sad desultory the way families and people sorta scatter around a beach and look vaguely at the sea, all disorganized and picnic sad—At one point I'm telling Evelyn that a tidal wave from Hawaii could very easily come someday and we'd see it miles away a huge wall of awful water and "Boy it would take some doing to run back and climb up these cliffs, huh?" but Cody hears this and says, "What?" and I say "It would wash over us and take us all to Salinas I bet" and Cody says "What? that brand new jeep? I'm goin back and move it!" (an example of his strange humor).

"How'd'st rain rule here?" says I to Evelyn to show her what a big poet I am—She really loves me, used to love me in the old days like a husband, for awhile there she had two husbands Cody and me, we were a perfect family till Cody finally got jealous or maybe I got jealous, it was wild for awhile I'd be coming home from work on the railroad all dirty with my lamp and just as I came in for my Joy bubblebath old Cody was rushing off on a call so Evelyn had her new husband in the second shift then when Cody come home at dawn all dirty for his Joy bubblebath, ring, the phone's run and the crew clerk's asked me out and I'm rushing off to work, both of us using the same old clunker car in shifts—And Evelyn always maintaining that she and I were really made for each other but her Karma was to serve Cody in this particular lifetime, which I really believe and I believe she loves him, too, but she'd say "I'll get you, Jack, in another lifetime . . . And you'll be very happy"—"What?" I'd yell to joke, "me running up the eternal halls of Karma tryina get away from you hey?"—"It'll take you eternities to get rid of me," she adds sadly, which makes me jealous, I want her to say I'll never get rid of her—I wanta be chased for eternity till I catch her.

"Ah Jack" she says putting her arm around me on the beach, "it's nice to see you again, Oh I wish we could be quiet again and just have our suppers of homemade pizza all together and watch T.V. together, you have so many friends and responsibilities now it's sad, and you get sick drinking and everything, why dont you just come stay with us awhile and rest"—"I will"—But Ron Blake is redhot for Evelyn and keeps coming over to dance with seaweeds and impress her, he's even asked me to ask Cody to let him spend some time alone with Evelyn, Cody's said "Go ahead man."

Having run out of liquor in fact Ron does get his opportunity to be alone with Evelyn as Cody and me and the kids in one car, and McLear and family in the other start for Monterey to stock up for the night and also more cigarettes—Evelyn and Ron light a bonfire on the beach to wait for us—As we're driving along little Timmy says to Paw "We shoulda brought Mommy with us, her pants got wet in the beach"—"By now they oughta be steamin," says Cody matter-of-factly in another one of his fantastic puns as he lockwallops that awful narrow dirt canyon road like a getaway car in the mountains in a movie, we leave poor McLear miles back—When Cody comes to a narrow tight curve with all our death staring us in the face down that hole he just swerves the curve saying "The way to drive in the mountains is, boy, no fiddlin around, these roads dont move, you're the one that moves"—And we come out on the highway and go right battin up to Monterey in the Big Sur dusk where down there on the faint gloamy frothing rocks you can hear the seals cry.

24

MCLEAR EXHIBITS ANOTHER STRANGE FACET of his handsome but
faintly "decaden" Rimbaud-type personality at his summer camp by
coming out in the livingroom with a goddamn HAWK on his shoulder—It's his pet hawk, of all things, the hawk is black as night and sits
there on his shoulder pecking nastily at a clunk of hamburg he holds
up to it—In fact the sight of that is so rarely poetic, McLear whose
poetry is really like a black hawk, he's always writing about darkness, dark brown, dark bedrooms, moving curtains, chemical fire
dark pillows, love in chemical fiery red darkness, and writes all that
in beautiful long lines that go across the page irregularly and aptly
somehow—Handsome Hawk McLear, in fact I suddenly yell out "Now
I know your real name! it's M'Lear! M' Lear the Scotch Highland
moorhaunter with his hawk about to go mad and tear his white hair
in a tempest"—Or some such silly thing, feeling good again now we've
got new wine—Time to go back to the cabin and fly down that dark
highway the way only Cody can fly (even bettern Dave Wain but you
feel safer with Dave Wain tho the reason Cody gives you a sense of
dooming boom as he pushes the night out the wheels is not because
he'll lose perfect control of the car but you feel the car will take off
suddenly up to Heaven or at least just up into what the Russians call
the Dark Cosmos, there's a booming rushing sound out the window
when Cody bats her down the white line at night, with Dave Wain
it's all conversation and smooth sailing, with Cody it's a crisis about
to get worse)—And now he's saying to me "Not only today but the
other day with the boys, that beautiful McLear woman there, wow,
with her tight blue jeans, man I cried under a tree to see that poppin
around so innocent like, whoo, so I tell you what we're gonna do old
buddy: tomorrow we go back to Los Gatos the whole family and we've
dropped Evelyn and the kids home after the hiss-the-villain play we're
all gonna see at seven—"—"The what?"—"It's a play," he says suddenly

imitating the tired whiney voice of an old P.T.A. Committee woman, "you go there and you sit down and out comes this old 1910 play about villains foreclosing the mortgage, mustaches, you know, calico tears, you can sit there you see and hiss the villain all you want even for all I know yell obscenities or something I dunno—But it's Evelyn's world, you know, she's designing the sets and that's the work she's done while I was in the can so I cant begrudge her that, in fact I aint got a word in edgewise, when you're the father of a family you go along with the little woman acourse, and the kids enjoy it, after that plan and after you've hissed the villain we'll drop them home and then old buddy" zooming up the car even of all thinks, the hawk is black as night and sits there faster in lieu of rubbing his hands with zeal, so to say Zoom, "you and me gonna go flyin down that Bay Shore highway and as usual you're gonna ask your usual dumb almost Okie wino ques- tions, *Hey Cody*" (whining like a old drunk) "*I b'lieve we're comin into Burlingame aint it*? and you're always wrong, hee hee, old crazy dumb fuckin old Jack, then we go rubbin shoulders into that City and go poppin right up to my sweet little old baby Willamine that I want you to meet inasmuch and also I want you go dig because she's gonna dig YOU my dear old sonumbitch Jack, and I'm gonna leave you two little lovebirds together for days on end alone, you can live there and just enjoy that gone little woman because also" (his tone now businesslike) "I want her to dig as much as possible everything you got to tell her about what YOU know, hear me? she's my soulmate and confidante and mistress and I want her to be happy and learn"—"What's she look like?" I ask grossly—And I see the grimace on his face, he really knows me, "Eh well she looks alright, she has a gone little body that's all I can say and in bed she is by far the first and only and last possible greatest everything you dig"—This being just another of a long line of occasions when Cody gets me to be a sub-beau for his beauties so that everything can tie in together, he really loves me like a brother and more than that, he gets annoyed at me sometimes especially when I fumble and blumble like with a bottle or the time I almost stripped the gears of the car because I forgot I was driving, in which case actu- ally I remind him of his old wino father but the fantastic thing is that HE reminds ME of MY father so that we have this strange eternal father-image relationship that goes on and on sometimes with tears, it's easy for me to think of Cody and almost cry, sometimes I can see the same tearful expression in his eyes when he sometimes looks at me—He reminds me of my father because he too blusters and hurries and fills all his pockets with Racing Forms and papers and pencils and we're all ready to go on some mission in the night he takes with ultimate seriousness as tho we were going on the last trip of them all but it always ends up being a hilarious meaningless Marx Brothers adventure which gives me even more reason to love him (and my father too)—That way—And finally in the book I wrote about us ("On The Road") I forgot to mention two important things, that we were both devout little Catholics in our childhood, which gives us something in common tho we never talk about it, it's just there in our natures, and secondly and most important that strange business when we shared another girl (Marylou, or that is, let's call her Joanna) and Cody at the time announced "That's what we'll be old buddy, you and me, double husbands, later on we'll have whole Harreeeem and reams of Hareems boy, and we'll call ourselves or that is" (flutter) "ourself Duluomeray, see Duluoz and Pomeray, Duluomeray, see, hee hee hee" tho he was younger then and really silly but that gives an indication of the way he felt about me: some kind of new thing in the world actually where men can really be angelic friends and not be homosexual and not fight over girls—But alas the only thing we'd ever fought about was money, or the ridiculous time we fought about a little line of marijuana dust running down the middle of a page where we were separating our shares with a knife, when I objected I wanted some of the dust he yelled "Our original agreement had nothing to do with the dust!" and he slumps it all into his pocket and stalks off redfaced so I jump up and pack and announce I'm leaving and Evelyn drives me to the City but the car wont start (this is years ago) so Cody redfaced and crazy and ashamed now has to push us with the clunker, there we go down San Jose boulevard with Cody behind us pushing us and with Cody behind us pushing us and bumping us not just to give us a start but to chastise me for being so greedy and I shouldnt leave at all—In fact he'd back up and come up on our rear and really wham us—That night ending me dead drunk on Mal Damlette's floor on

North Beach—And in any case the whole question of us, the two most advanced men friends in the world still fighting over money after all being, as Julien says in New York, indication of the fact that "Money is the only thing Canucks ever fight about, and Okies too I guess" but Julien I suppose imagining and fantasizing himself as a noble Scotsman who fights about honor (tho I tell him "Ah you Scotchmen save your spit in your watchpocket").

Lacrimae rerum, the tears of things, all the years behind me and Cody, the way I always say "me and Cody" instead of "Cody and I" or some such, and Irwin watching us across the world night now with a bite of marvel on his lower lip saying "Ah, angels of the West, Companions in Heaven" and writing letters asking "What now, what's the latest, what visions, what arguments, what sweet agreements?" and such.

That night the kids end up sleeping in the jeep anyway because they're afraid of the big black woods and I sleep by the creek in my bag and in the morning we're all set to go back to Los Gatos and see the villain play—Frustrated Ron is casting sad eyes at Evelyn, apparently she's put him off because she says to me (and I dont blame her) "Really the way Cody presses people on me it's awful, at least I should have my own choice" (but she's laughing because it's funny and it is funny the way Cody does it anxious and harried wondering if that's what she really wants and wants no such thing)—"At least not with utter strangers," says I to be funny—She:-"Besides I'm so sick of all this sex business, that's all he talks about, his friends, here they are all open channels to do good as co creators with God and all they think about is behinds—that's why you're so refreshing" she adds—"But I aint so refreshing as all that? hey!"—But that's my relationship with Evelyn, we're real pals and we can kid about anything even the first night I met her in Denver in 1947 when we danced and Cody watched anxiously, a kind of romantic pair in fact and I shudder sometimes to think of all that stellar mystery of how she IS going to get me in a future lifetime, wow—And I seriously do believe that will be my salvation, too.

A long way to go.

25

THE SILLY STUPID hiss-the-villian play is alright in itself but just as we arrive at the scene of the chuck wagons and tents all done up real old western style there's a big fat sheriff type with two sixshooters standing at the admission gate, Cody says "That's to give it color see" but I'm drunk and as we all pile out of the car I go up to the fat sheriff and start telling him a Southern joke (in fact just the plot of an Erskine Caldwell short story) which he receives with a witless smiling expression or really like the expression of an executioner or a Southern constable listening to a Yankee talk—So naturally I'm surprised later when we go into the cute old west saloon and the kids start banging on the old piano and I join them with big loud Stravinsky chords, here comes two gun sheriff fatty coming in and saying in a menacing voice like T.V. western movies "You cant play that piano"—I'm surprised, turning to Evelyn, to learn that he's the blasted proprietor of the whole place and if he says I cant play the piano there's nothing I can do about it legally—But besides that he's got actual bullets in those six guns—He's going all out to play the part—But to be yanked from joyful pianothumping with kids to see that awful dead face of negative horror I just jump up and say "Alright, the hell with it I'm leaving anyway" so Cody follows me to the car where I take another swig of white port—"Let's get the hell out of here" I say—"Just what I was thinkin about," says Cody, "in fact I've already arranged with the director of the play to drive Evelyn and the kids home so we'll just go to the City now"—"Great!"—"And I've told Evelyn we're cuttin out so let's go."

"I'm sorry Cody I screwed up your little family party"—"No No" he protests "Man I have to come to these things you know and be a big hubby and father type and you know I'm on parole and I gotta put up appearances but it's a drag"—To show what a drag it is we go scootin down that road passing six cars easy as pie—"And I'm GLAD this happened because it gave us an excuse, hee hee titter you know to get outa there, I was thinking for an excuse when it happened, that old fart is crazy you know! he's a millionaire you know! I've talked to him, that little beady brain, and you be glad you missed hangin around till that performance, man, and that AUDIENCE, ow, ugh, I almost wish I was back in San Quentin but here we go, son!"

So of old we're alone in a car at night bashing down the line to a specific somewhere, nothing nowhere about it whatever, especially this time, in a way—That white line is feeding into our fender like an anxious impatient electronic quiver shuddering in the night and how beautifully sometimes it curves one side or the other as he smoothly swerves for passing or for something else, avoiding a bump or something—And on the big highway Bay Shore how beautifully he just swings in and out of lanes almost effortlessly and completely unnoticeable passing to the right and to the left without a flaw all kinds of cars with anxious eyes turning to us, altho he's the only one on the road who knows how to drive completely well—It's blue dusk all up and down the California world—Frisco glitters up ahead—Our radio plays rhythm and blues as we pass the joint back and forth in jutjawed silence both looking ahead with big private thoughts now so vast we cant communicate them any more and if we tried it would take a million years and a billion books—Too late, too late, the history of everything we've seen together and separately has become a library in itself—The shelves pile higher—They're full of misty documents or documents of the Mist—The mind has convoluted in every tuckaway everywhichaway tuckered hole till there's no more the expressing of our latest thoughts let alone old—Mighty genius of the mind Cody whom I announce as the greatest writer the world will ever know if he ever gets down to writing again like he did earlier—It's so enormous we both sit here sighing in fact—"No the only writing I done," he says, "a few letters to Willamine, in fact quite a few, she's got em all wrapped in ribbons there, I figgered if I tried to write a book or sumptin or prose or sumptin they'd just take it away from me when I left so I wrote her 'bout three letters a week for two years—and the trouble of course and as I say and you've heard a million times is the mind flows the mind rises and nobody can by any possible c—oh hell,

I dont wanta talk about it"—Besides I can see from glancing at him
that becoming a writer holds no interest for him because life is so
holy for him there's no need to do anything but live it, writing's just
an afterthought or a scratch anyway at the surface—But if he could!
if he would! there I am riding in California miles away from home
where my poor cat's buried and my mother grieves and that's what
I'm thinking.

   It always makes me proud to love the world somehow—Hate's so
easy compared—But here I go flattering myself helling headbent to
the silliest hate I ever had.

26

ALTHO CODY'S SAID THESE THINGS I'm very well aware that the real arrangement of the evening is that we're just going to see Billie together so she can get her kicks meeting me (after hearing about me from him and after reading my books etc.) and in fact Cody has already conferred with Evelyn about how I'm going to be staying at their house in Las Gatos for a month, as of old sleeping in my bag in the backyard not because they dont want me to sleep in the house but it's my idea, but it's beautiful anyway to sleep under the stars and anyway I therefore keep out of the way of the family when they get up to go to work and school—At noon they see me shambling in from the big back field yard yawning for coffee—And I'm in line for that, i.e., that's what I want to do and that's my plan—But when we run upstairs to Willamine's apartment and come bursting in to this neat little well arranged pad with goldfish bowl, books, strange doo-dads, neat kitchen, the whole clean as a pin, and there's Billie herself a blonde with arched eyebrows exactly like the male Julien blond with arched eyebrows and I yell out "It's JUlien by God it's Julien!" (and by now I'm drunk anyway because we've as of old picked up an old hitch hiker on Bay Shore who says his name is Joe Ihnat and we bought him a bottle and I bought me one too, never will forget old Joe Ihnat in fact somehow because he said he was a Russian and his was an ancient Russian name and when I wrote out our names he said *my* name was an ancient Russian name also) (tho it's Breton) (and also told us he'd just been beaten up by a young Negro for no reason in a public toilet and Cody gasps and says to me "I've met those Negroes that beat up old men, they're called the Strongarms in San Quentin, they're all put away among themselves away from the other prisoners, they're all Negroes and it seems all they wanta do is beat up old defenseless men, he's tellin the absolute truth"—"But why do they do that?"—"Oh man I dont know they just wanta hit up on some old man that cant hit

back and just beat him and beat him till he's dead" and Oh the horror
of Cody's knowledge of the world when all is said and done)—So now
we're sitting with Billie in her pad, outside the window you see the
glittering lights of the city again, ah Urbi y Roma, the world again,
and she's got these mad blue eyes, arched eyebrows, intelligent face,
just like Julien, I keep saying "Julien goddamit!" and I see even in
my drunkenness a little worried flutter in Cody's eyes—The fact of
the matter being, Billie and I go for each other like two tons of bricks
right there in front of Cody so that when he rises and announces he's
going back to Los Gatos to get some sleep to go to work it's already
well agreed I'm staying right where I am and not only for tonight but
for weeks months years.

    Poor Cody—Yet you see I've already explained why actually sub-
consciously this is what he really wants to happen but he wont admit
it ever and always invents reasons around this to get mad at me and
call me a bastard—But aside from Cody I find Billie to be a very com-
panionable strange kid in this lonesome night and I actually NEED
to stay with her awhile—In fact both Billie and I explain to Cody
why—But there's nothing evil, man-against-man or sinister about
any of it, it's just a strange innocence, a spontaneous burst of love in
fact and Cody understands that bettern anybody else anyway so he
leaves at midnight saying he'll be back tomorrow night and all of a
sudden I'm alone with a charming woman and we're talking a blue
streak sitting crosslegged facing each other on the floor in a litter of
books and bottles.

    It gives me a pang of pain and remorse really now to recall that on
this first night her apartment was so neat and clean and charming—
The chair by the goldfish bowl which I quickly appropriated as my
old man chair, where I sat constantly sipping port for a whole week,
the kitchen with its intelligent arrangements of spices and eggs in the
icebox, and for that matter too the poor little son of Billie sleeping in
a well arranged back room (her son from her deceased husband who
was also a railroad man)—Elliott the child's name and I didnt get to
see him till later that night—And with the huge packet of Cody's San
Quentin letters in her hand she launches forth on her theories about
Cody and eternity but all I can keep saying as I swig from my bottle

is "Julien, you're talking too much! Julien, Julien, my God who'd ever dream I'd run into a woman who looks like Julien . . . you look like Julien but you're not Julien and on top of that you're a woman, how goddam strange"—In fact she had to pack me off to bed drunk—But not before our first lovely undertaking of love and everything Cody said about her being absolutely true—But the main thing being that tho she looked like Julien etc. and had Cody's big sad abstract letters about Karma in a ribbon and actually went out in the morning and earned a hundred a week in fashion modeling she had the most musical beautiful and sad voice I've ever heard in my life—The things she's saying are really rather inane because after all her education is based on really Californian hysterias like the earlier mistress of Cody Rosemarie who also was thin and pale haired and crazy and kept talking abstract—(Like she's saying "I thought I could do something to ease the contradiction between immanent and universal ethics which I thought was my problem and was what I hoped to gain thru therapy, like, any evolution presupposes an involution and all that kind of thinking" as I sigh, but she does say something interesting once in a while like "While Cody was in prison my main occupation was praying for him, I had an all day going, there was also a bit we did together every evening from 9:00 to 9:09 but he's out now and something else is happening I'm not sure what . . . but I'm sure we aid the storm when we transcend time in one respect and cant even keep up with it in others. . .")—But also all kinds of to-me-unimportant and uninteresting crap about channels about people being either closed or open channels and Cody is a big open channel pouring out all his holy gysm on Heaven, I really cant remember, or the destinies, the sighs, the rooftops of all that, the stars are shining down on their poor heads as they draw breath to explain inanities really—Like the letters to her (I glance at them) are all about how they've met and their souls have collided in this dimension because of some unfulfilled Karma on another planet and in another plane that is, and now they have to gird themselves to assume this big responsibility to meet some measure of this and that, I dont even wanta go into it—Because also the fact of the matter being, when Willamine talks to me I'm utterly bored, I'm only interested in the sad music of her voice and in the strange circumstance (I guess Karmalike too) that she looks like poor Julien.

Her voice is the main point—She talks with a broken heart—Her voice lutes brokenly like a heart lost, musically too, like in a lost grove, it's almost too much to bear sometimes like some fantastic futuristic Jerry Southern singer in a night club who steps up to the mike in the spotlight in Las Vegas but doesnt even have to sing, just talk, to make men sigh and women wonder I guess (if women ever wonder)—So that as she's trying to explain all that nonsense to me (all that philosophy of hers and Cody's and Cody's new buddy Perry, coming up the next day) I just sit and marvel and stare at her mouth wondering where all the beauty is coming from and why—And we end up making love sweetly too—A little blonde well experienced in all the facets of lovemaking and sweet with compassion and just too much so that b'dawn we're already going to get married and fly away to Mexico in a week—In fact I can see it now, a great big four way marriage with Cody and Evelyn.

For she is the great enemy of Evelyn—She's not satisfied just to be Cody's lover and soul heart she wants to go right over there and lay Evelyn down on the line and take Cody away with her forever and to do this she'll even have a deadend heaven deep love affair with old Jack (same pattern of old)—There's not much difference between her and Evelyn when you listen to their talk about Cody except in Evelyn's case I'm always fascinatedly interested—Billie actually bores me tho of course I cant tell her that—Evelyn is still the champ and I wonder about Cody.

O the ups and downs and juggling of women, blondes at that, all in the great magical City of the Gandharvas of San Francisco and here I am alone on a magic carpet with one of em, whee, at first of course it's a great ball, a great new eye-shattering explosion of experience—Not dreaming, I, what's to come—For with sad musical Billie in my arms and my name Billie too now, Billie and Billie arm in arm, oh beautiful, and Cody has given his consent in a way, we go roaming the Genghiz Khan clouds of soft love and hope and anybody who's never done this is crazy—Because a new love affair always gives hope, the irrational mortal loneliness is always crowned, that thing I saw (that horror of snake emptiness) when I took the deep iodine deathbreath on the

Big Sur beach is now justified and hosannah'd and raised up like a
sacred urn to Heaven in the mere fact of the taking off of clothes and
clashing wits and bodies in the inexpressibly nervously sad delight
of love—Dont let no old fogies tell you otherwise, and on top of that
nobody in the world even ever dares to write the true story of love,
it's awful, we're stuck with a 50% incomplete literature and drama—
Lying mouth to mouth, kiss to kiss in the pillow dark, loin to loin in
unbelievable surrendering sweetness so distant from all our mental
fearful abstractions it makes you wonder why men have termed God
antisexual somehow—The secret underground truth of mad desire
hiding under fenders under buried junkyards throughout the world,
never mentioned in newspapers, written about haltingly and like corn
by authors and painted tongue in cheek by artists, agh, just listen to
Tristan und Isolde by Wagner and think of him in a Bavarian field
with his beloved naked beauty under the fall leaves.

How strange in all, and making everything that's happened in the
past weeks, the backs and forths and pains of me in City and Sur, all
piled up now rationally like a big construction whereon could be built
a divingboard which would enable me clumsily to dive into Billie's
soul and therefore why complain?

In the middle of the night she fetches the little 4 year old boy to
show me the spiritual beauty of her son—He is one of the weirdest
persons I've ever met—He has large liquid brown eyes very beautiful
and he hates anybody who comes near his mother and keeps asking
her questions constantly like "Why do you stay with him? why is he
here, who is he?" or "Why is it dark outside?" or "Why does the sun
shine yesterday?" or anything, he'll just ask questions about everything and she answers every one of them with extreme delight and
patience till I say "Doesnt he bother you with all these questions?
why dont you let him croon and goof like a little child, he's tugging
at your knee asking EVERYTHING man why dont you just let him
singsong?"—She answers "I answer him because I may be missing his
next question, everything he asks me and says to me represents something important about the absolute I may be missing"—"What do you
mean the absolute?"—"You yourself said everything is the absolute"
but of course she's right and I realize that in my dirty old soul I'm
already jealous of Elliott.

27

THE MAT OF NIGHT admits the groaning glory godlike love I guess but at the same time it's also boring in a way and we both laugh to discuss that—We stay awake that first night till dawn discussing everything in the books from Cody in every detail down to me in every detail to her in every detail to Evelyn to books and philosophies and religions and the absolute and I end up whispering her poems—Poor kid has to get up in the morning and go to work and I'm left there snoring drunk—But she makes her neat breakfast and takes Elliott off to the daily babysitter lady and I wake up at one in the afternoon alone and take a swig of wine and get in the hot bath to read a book—The phone keeps ringing, everybody from Monsanto to Fagan to McLear to the Moon Man has somehow found out where I am and what the number is, tho none of them have previously even met Billie let alone seen her—I shudder to realize Cody will get mad for making his secret life so public.

But here comes Perry—Like me Perry has that strange brotherly relationship with Cody whereby he gets to be *confidant* and sometimes lover of all Cody's gals—And I can see why—He looks just like me only he's young and looks like I did when first Cody met me but the point is not that so much, he is a tempestuous lost tossed soul just out of Soledad State Prison for attempted robbery with a boyish face and black hair falling over it but powerful thick muscular arms that I realize he could break a man in half with—His name is strange too, Perry Yturbide, I immediately say: "I know what you are, Basque"— "Basque? is that it? I never found out! let's call my mother longdistance in Utah and tell her that!"—And he rings up his mother way over there, on Billie's phone bill, and here I am bottle of port wine in one hand and butt in mouth talking to a Basque ex con's mother in Utah telling her in fact reassuring her "Yes I believe it's a Basque name"—She's saying "Hey, what you say? who are you?" and there's

Perry smiling all glad—A very strange kid—It's been a long time in
fact in my literary sort of life that I've met a real tough hombre like
that out of jails and with those arms of steel and that fevered concern that scares governments and makes officials pale, that's why he's
always put away in prison this type of man—Yes yet the type of man
the country always needs when there's a little old war started by an
aging governor—A real dangerous character, in fact, Perry, because
tho I appreciate his poetic soul and everything I realize looking at
him he's capable of exploding and killing somebody for an idea maybe
or for love.

Some of his own friends ring Billie's doorbell, everybody seems to
know I'm there, they come up, they are strange anarchistic Negroes
and ex cons, it seems to be some sort of gang, I begin to wonder—Like
a ring of fevered sages, the Negroes are intense and crazy and intellectual but they've all got those strong muscular arms again and all have
jail records yet they all talk as tho the end of the world depended on
their words—Hard to explain (but will do).

Billie and her gang in fact, with all that fancy rigamarole about
spiritual matters I wonder if it isnt just a big secret hustler outfit tho
I also realize that I've noticed it before in San Francisco a kind of
ephemeral hysteria that hides in the air over the rooftops among
certain circles there leading always to suicide and maim—Me just
an innocent lost hearted meditator and Goop among strange intense
criminal agitators of the heart—It reminds me in fact of a nightmare I
had just before coming out to the Coast, in the dream I'm back in San
Francisco but there's something funny going on: there's dead silence
throughout the entire city: men like printers and office executives and
housepainters are all standing silently in second floor windows looking down on the empty streets of San Francisco: once in a while some
beatniks walk by below, also silent: they're being watched but not only
by the authorities but by everybody: the beatniks seem to have the
whole street system to themselves: but nobody's saying anything: and
in this intense silence I take a ride on a self propelled platform right
downtown and out to the farms where a woman running a chicken
farm invites me to join her and live with her—The little platform
rolling quietly as the people are watching from windows in groups of

profile like the profiles in old Van Dyck paintings, intense, suspicious, momentous—This Billie business reminding me of that but because to me the only thing that matters is the conceptions in my own mind, there has to be no reality anyway to what I suppose is going on—But this also an indication of the coming madness in Big Sur.

28

STRANGE—and Perry Yturbide that first day while Billie's at work and we've just called his mother now wants me to come with him to visit a general of the U.S. Army—"Why? and what's all these generals looking out of silent windows?" I say—But nothing surprises Perry— "Well go there because I want you to dig the most beautiful girls we ever saw," in fact we take a cab—But the "beautiful girls" turn out to be 8 and 9 and 10 years old, daughters of the general or maybe even cousins or daughters of a nextdoor strange general, but the mother is there, there are also boys playing in a backroom, we have Elliott with us whom Perry has carried on his shoulders all the way—I look at Perry and he says "I wanted you to see the most beautiful little cans in town" and I realize he's dangerously insane—In fact he then says "See this perfect beauty?" a pony tailed 10 year old daughter of the general (who aint home yet) "I'm going to kidnap her right now" and he takes her by the hand and they go out on the street for an hour while I sit there over drinks talking to the mother—There's some vast conspiracy to make me go mad anyway—The mother is polite as ordinarily—The general comes home and he's a rugged big bald-headed general and with him is his best friend a photographer called Shea, a thin well combed welldressed ordinary downtown commercial photographer of the city—I dont understand anything—But suddenly little Elliott is crying in the other room and I rush in there and see that the two boys have whacked him or something because he did something wrong so I chastise them and carry Elliott back into the livingroom on my shoulders like Perry does, only Elliott wants to get down off my shoulders at once, in fact he wont even sit on my lap, in fact he hates my guts—I call Billie desperately at her agency and she says she'll be over to pick us all up and adds "How's Perry today?"—"He's kidnapping little girls he says are beautiful, he wants to marry 10 year old girls with pony tails"—"That's the way he is, be sure to dig him"—In her musical sad voice over the phone.

I turn my poor tortured attention to the general who says he was an anti-Fascist fighter with the Maquis during World War II and also a guerilla in the South Pacific and knows one of the finest restaurants in San Francisco where we can all go feast, a Fillipino restaurant near Chinatown, I say okay, great—He gives me more booze—Seeing the amusing Irish face of Shea the photographer I yell "You can take my picture anytime you want" and he says sinister: "Not for propaganda reasons, anything but propaganda reasons"—"What the hell do you mean propaganda reasons, I aint got nothin to do with propaganda" (and here comes Perry back through the door with Poopoo holding his hand, they've gone to dig the street and have a coke) and I realize everybody is just living their lives quietly but it's only me that's insane.

In fact I yearn to have old Cody around to explain all this to me tho it soon becomes apparent to me not even Cody could explain, I'm beginning to go seriously crazy, just like Subterranean Irene went crazy tho I dont realize it yet—I'm beginning to read plots into every simple line—Besides the "general" scares me even further by turning out to be a strange affluent welldressed civilian who doesnt even help me to pay the tab for the Fillipino dinner which we have, meeting Billie at the restaurant, and the restaurant itself is weird especially because of a big raunchy mad thicklipped sloppy young Fillipino woman sitting alone at the end of the restaurant gobbling up her food obscenely and looking at us insolently as tho to say "Fuck you, I eat the way I like" splashing gravy everywhere—I cant understand what's going on—Because also the general has suggested this dinner but I have to pay for everybody, him, Shea, Perry, Billie, Elliott, me, others, strange apocalyptic madness is now shuddering in my eyeballs and I'm even running out of money in their Apocalypse which they themselves have created in this San Francisco silence anyway.

I yearn to go hide and cry in Evelyn's arms but I end up hiding in Billie's arms and here she goes again, the second evening, explaining all her spiritual ideas—"But what about Perry? what's he up to? and who's that strange general? what are you, a bunch of communists?"

29

THE LITTLE CHILD REFUSES to sleep in his crib but has to come trotting out and watch us make love on the bed but Billie says "That's good, he'll learn, what other way will he ever learn?"—I feel ashamed but because Billie is there and she's the mother I must go along and not worry—Another sinister fact—At one point the poor child is drooling long slavers of spit from his lips watching, I cry "Billie, look at him, it's not good for him" but she says again "Anything he wants he can have, *even us.*"

"But kid it's not fair, why doesn't he just sleep?"—"He doesnt wanta sleep, he wants to be with us"—"Ooh," and I realize Billie is insane and I'm not as insane as I thought and there's something wrong—I feel my self skidding: also because during the following week I keep sitting in that same chair by the goldfish bowl drinking bottle after bottle of port like an automaton, worrying about something, Monsanto comes to visit, McLear, Fagan, everybody, they call to me dashing up the stairs and we have long drunken days talking but I never seem to get out of that chair and never even take another delightful warm bath reading books—And at night Billie comes home and we pitch into love again like monsters who dont know what else to do and by now I'm too blurry to know what's going on anyway tho she reassures me everything is alright, and meanwhile Cody has completely disappeared—In fact I call him up and say "Are you gonna come back and get me here?"—"Yes yes yes in a few days, stay there" as tho maybe he wants me to learn what's happening like putting me through an ordeal to see what I have to say about it because he's been through the ordeal himself.

In fact everything is going crazy.

Perry's visits scare me: I begin to think he must be one of those "strong armers" who beat up old men: I watch him warily—All this time he's pacing back and forth saying "Man dont you appreciate those sweet little cans? what does it matter how old a woman is, 9 or 19, those little pony tails jiggling as they walk with those little jigglin cans"—"Did you ever kidnap one?"—"You out of wine, I'll make a run for you get some more, or would you rather have pot or sumptin? what's wrong with you?"—"I dont know what's goin on!"—"You're drinking too much maybe, Cody told me you're falling apart man, dont do it"—"But what's goin on?"—"Who cares, pops, we're all swingin in love and tryin to go from day to day with self respect while all the squares are puttin us down"—"Who?"—"The Squares, puttin down Us . . . we wanta swing and live and carry across the night like when we get to L.A. I'm goin to show you the maddest scene some friends of mine down there" (in my drunkenness I've already projected a big trip with Billie and Elliott and Perry to Mexico but we're going to stop in L.A. to see a rich woman Perry knows who's going to give him money and if she doesnt he's going to get it anyway, and as I say Billie and I are going to get married too)—The insanest week of my life—Billie at night saying "You're worried that I cant handle marrying you but of course we can, Cody wants it too, I'll talk to your mother and make her love me and need me: Jack!" she suddenly cries with anguished musical voice (because I've just said "Ah Billie go get yourself a he-man and get married"), "You're my last chance to marry a He Man"—"Whattayou mean He Man, dont you realize I'm crazy?"—"You're crazy but you're my last chance to have an understanding with a He Man"—"What about Cody?"—"Cody will never leave Evelyn"—Very strange—But more, tho I dont understand it.

30

I DO UNDERSTAND THE STRANGE day Ben Fagan finally came to visit me alone, bringing wine, smoking his pipe, and saying "Jack you need some sleep, that chair you say you've been sitting in for days have you noticed the bottom is falling out of it?"—I get on the floor and by God look and it's true, the springs are coming out—"How long have you been sitting in that chair?"—"Every day waiting for Billie to come home and talking to Perry and the others all day. . . My God let's go out and sit in the park," I add—In the blur of days McLear has also been over on a forgotten day when, on nothing but his chance mention that maybe I could get his book published in Paris I jump up and dial longdistance for Paris and call Claude Gallimard and only get his butler apparently in some Parisian suburb and I hear the insane giggle on the other end of the line—"Is this the home, *c'est le chez eux de Monsieur Gallimard?*"—Giggle—"*Où est Monsieur Gallimard?*"—Giggle—A very strange phone call—McLear waiting there expectantly to get his "Dark Brown" published—So in a fury of madness I then call London to talk to my old buddy Lionel just for no reason at all and I finally reach him at home he's saying on the wire "You're calling me from San Francisco? but why?"—Which I cant answer any more than the giggling butler (and to add to my madness, of course, why should a longdistance call to Paris to a publisher end up with a giggle and a longdistance call to an old friend in London end up with the friend getting mad?)—So Fagan now sees I'm going overboard crazy and I need sleep—"We'll get a bottle!" I yell—But end up, he's sitting in the grass of the park smoking his pipe, from noon to 6 P.M., and I'm passed out exhausted sleeping in the grass, bottle unopened, only to wake up once in a while wondering where I am and by God I'm in Heaven with Ben Fagan watching over men and me.

And I say to Ben when I wake up in the gathering 6 P.M. dusk "Ah Ben I'm sorry I ruined our day by sleeping like this" but he says: "You needed the sleep, I told ya"—"And you mean to tell me you been sitting all afternoon like that?"—"Watching unexpected events," says he, "like there seems to be sound of a Bacchanal in those bushes over there" and I look and hear children yelling and screaming in hidden bushes in the park—"What they doing?"—"I dont know: also a lot of strange people went by"—"How long have I been sleeping?"—"Ages"—"I'm sorry"—"Why should be sorry, I love you anyway"—"Was I snoring?"—"You've been snoring all day and I've been sitting here all day"—"What a beautiful day!"—"Yes it's been a beautiful day"—"How strange!"—"Yes, strange . . . but not so strange either, you're just tired"—"What do you think of Billie?"—He chuckles over his pipe: "What do you expect me to say? that the frog bit your leg?"—"Why do you have a diamond in your forehead?"—"I dont have a diamond in my forehead damn you and stop making arbitrary conceptions!" he roars—"But what am I doing?"—"Stop thinking about yourself, will ya, just float with the world"—"Did the world float by the park?"—"All day, you should have seen it, I've smoked a whole package of Edgewood, it's been a very strange day"—"Are you sad I didnt talk to you?"—"Not at all, in fact I'm glad: we better be starting back," he adds, "Billie be coming home from work soon now"—"Ah Ben, Ah Sunflower"—"Ah shit" he says—"It's strange"—"Who said it wasnt"—"I dont understand it"—"Dont worry about it"—"Hmm holy room, sad room, life is a sad room"—"All sentient beings realize that," he says sternly—Benjamin my real Zen Master even more than all our Georges and Arthurs actually—"Ben I think I'm going crazy"—"You said that to me in 1955"—"Yeh but my brain's gettin soft from drinkin and drinkin and drinkin"—"What you need is a cup of tea I'd say if I didnt know that you're too crazy to know how really crazy you are"—"But why? what's going on?"—"Did you come three thousand miles to find out?"—"Three thousand miles from where, after all? from whiney old me"—"That's alright, everything is possible, even Nietzsche knew that"—"Aint nothin wrong with old Nietzsche"—"'Xcept he went mad too"—"Do you think I'm going mad?"—"Ho ho ho" (hearty laugh)—"What's that mean, laughing at me?"—"Nobody's laughing at you, dont get excited"—"What'll we do now?"—"Let's go visit the museum over there"—There's a museum of some sort across

the grass of the park so I get up wobbly and walk with old Ben across
the sad grass, at one point I put my arm over his shoulder and lean
on him—"Are you a ghoul?" I ask—"Sure, why not?"—"I like ghouls
that let me sleep?"—"Duluoz it's good for you to drink in a way 'cause
you're awful stingy with yourself when You're sober"—"You sound
like Julien"—"I never met Julien but I understand Billie looks like
him, you kept saying that before you went to sleep"—"What happened
while I was asleep?"—"Oh, people went by and came back and forth
and the sun sank and finally sank down and's gone now almost as
you can see, what you want, just name it you got it"—"Well I want
sweet salvation"—"What's sposed to be sweet about salvation? maybe
it's sour"—"It's sour in my mouth"—"Maybe your mouth is too big,
or too small, salvation is for little kitties but only for awhile"—"Did
you see any little kitties today?"—"Shore, hundreds of em came to
visit you while you were sleeping"—"Really?"—"Sure, didnt you know
you were saved?"—"Now come on!"—"One of them was real big and
roared like a lion but he had a big wet snout and kissed you and you
said *Ah*"—"What's this museum up here?"—"Let's go in and find
out"—That's the way Ben is, he doesnt know what's going on either but
at least he waits to find out maybe—But the museum is closed—We
stand there on the steps looking at the closed door—"Hey," I say, "the
temple is closed."

So suddenly in red sundown me and Ben Fagan arm in arm are
walking slowly sadly back down the broad steps like two monks
going down the esplanade of Kyoto (as I imagine Kyoto somehow)
and we're both smiling happily suddenly—I feel good because I've had
my sleep but mainly I feel good because somehow old Ben (my age)
has blessed me by sitting over my sleep all day and now with these
few silly words—Arm in arm we slowly descend the steps without a
word—It's been the only peaceful day I've had in California, in fact,
except alone in the woods, which I tell him and says "Well, who said
you werent alone now?" making me realize the ghostliness of exis-
tence tho I feel his big bulging body with my hands and say: "You sure
some pathetic ghost with all that ephemeral heavy crock a flesh"—"I
didnt say nottin" he laughs—"Whatever I say Ben, dont mind it,
I'm just a fool"—"You said in 1957 in the grass drunk on whiskey

you were the greatest thinker in the world"—"That was before I fell asleep and woke up: now I realize I'm no good at all and that makes me feel free"—"You're not even free being no good, you better stop thinking, that's all"—"I'm glad you visited me today, I think I might have died"—"It's all your fault"—"What are we gonna do with our lives?"—"Oh," he says, "I dunno, just watch em I guess"—"Do you hate me? . . . well, do you like me? . . . well, how are things?"—"The hicks are alright"—"Anybody hex ya lately . . . ?"—"Yeh, with cardboard games?"—"Cardboard games?" I ask—"Well you know, they build cardboard houses and put people in them and the people are cardboard and the magician makes the dead body twitch and they bring water to the moon, and the moon has a strange ear, and all that, so I'm alright, Goof."

"Okay."

31

SO THERE I AM as it starts to get dark standing with one hand on the window curtain looking down on the street as Ben Fagan walks away to get the bus on the corner, his big baggy corduroy pants and simple blue Goodwill workshirt, going home to the bubble bath and a famous poem, not really worried or at least not worried about what I'm worried about tho he too carries that anguishing guilt I guess and hopeless remorse that the potboiler of time hasnt made his early primordial dawns over the pines of Oregon come true—I'm clutching at the drapes of the window like the Phantom of the Opera behind the masque, waiting for Billie to come home and remembering how I used to stand by the windows like this in my childhood and look out on dusky streets and think how awful I was in this development everybody said was supposed to be "my life" and "their lives."—Not so much that I'm a drunkard that I feel guilty about but that others who occupy this plane of "life on earth" with me dont feel guilty at all—Crooked judges shaving and smiling in the morning on the way to their heinous indifferences, respectable generals ordering soldiers by telephone to go die or drop dead, pickpockets nodding in cells saying "I never hurt anybody," "that's one thing you can say for me, yes sir," women who regard themselves saviors of men simply stealing their substance because they think their swan-rich necks deserve it anyway (though for every swan-rich neck you lose there's another ten waiting, each one ready to lay for a lemon), in fact awful hugefaced monsters of men just because their shirts are clean deigning to control the lives of working men by running for Governor saying "Your tax money in my hands will be aptly used," "You should realize how valuable I am and how much you need me, without me what would you be, not led at all?"—Forward to the big designed mankind cartoon of a man standing facing the rising sun with strong shoulders with a plough at his feet, the necktied governor is going to make hay while the sun rises—?—I feel guilty for being a member of the human race—Drunkard yes and one of the worst fools on earth—In fact not even a genuine drunkard just a fool—But I stand there with hand on curtain looking down for Billie, who's late, Ah me, I remember that frightening thing Milarepa said which is other than those reassuring words of his I remembered in the cabin of sweet loneness on Big Sur: "When the various experiences come to light in meditation, do not be proud and anxious to tell other people, else to Goddesses and Mothers you will bring annoyance" and here I am a perfectly obvious fool American writer doing just that not only for a living (which I was always able to glean anyway from railroad and ship and lifting boards and sacks with humble hand) but because if I dont write what actually I see happening in this unhappy globe which is rounded by the contours of my deathskull I think I'll have been sent on earth by poor God for nothing—Tho being a Phantom of the Opera why should that worry me?—In my youth leaning my brow hopelessly on the typewriter bar, wondering why God ever was anyway?—Or biting my lip in brown glooms in the parlor chair in which my father's died and we've all died a million deaths—Only Fagan can understand and now he's got his bus—And when Billie comes home with Elliott I smile and sit down in the chair and it utterly collapses under me, blang, I'm sprawled on the floor with surprise, the chair has gone.

"How'd that happen?" wonders Billie and at the same time we both look at the fishbowl and both the goldfishes are upsidedown floating dead on the surface of the water.

I've been sitting in that chair by that fishbowl for a week drinking and smoking and talking and now the goldfish are dead.

"What killed them?"—"I dont know"—"Did I kill the because I gave them some Kelloggs corn flakes?"—"Mebbe, you're not supposed to give them anything but their fish food"—"But I thought they were hungry so I gave them a few flicks of corn flakes"—"Well I dont know what killed them"—"But why dont anybody know? what happened? why do they do this? otters and mouses and every damn thing dyin on all sides Billie, I cant stand it, it's all my goddam fault every time!"— "Who said it was your fault dear?"—"Dear? you call me dear? why do you call me dear?"—"Ah, let me love you" (kissing me), "just because you dont deserve it"—(Chastised):- "Why dont I deserve it"—"Because you say so. . ."—"But what about the fish"—"I dont know, really"—"Is it because I've been sitting in that crumbling chair all week blowing smoke on their water? and all the others smoking and all the talk?"— But the little kid Elliott comes crawling up his mommy's lap and starts asking questions: "Billie," he calls her, "Billie, Billie, Billie," feeling her face, I'm almost going mad from the sadness of it all—"What did you do all day?"—"I was with Ben Fagan and slept in the park. . . Billie what are we gonna do?"—"Anytime you say like you said, we'll get married and fly to Mexico with Perry and Elliott"—"I'm afraid of Perry and I'm afraid of Elliott"—"He's only a little boy"—"Billie I dont wanta get married, I'm afraid. . ."—"Afraid?"—"I wanta go home and die with my cat." I could be a handsome thin young president in a suit sitting in an oldfashioned rocking chair, no instead I'm just the Phantom of the Opera standing by a drape among dead fish and broken chairs—Can it be that no one cares who made me or why?— "Jack what's the matter, what are you talking about?" but suddenly as she's making supper and poor little Elliott is waiting there with spoon upended in fist I realize it's just a little family home scene and I'm just a nut in the wrong place—And in fact Billie starts saying "Jack we should be married and have quiet suppers like this with Elliott, something would sanctify you forever I'm positive."

"What have I done wrong?"—"What you've done wrong is with-hold your love from a woman like me and from previous women and future women like me—can you imagine all the fun we'd have being married, putting Elliott to bed, going out to hear jazz or even taking planes to Paris suddenly and all the things I have to teach you and you teach me—instead all you've been doing is wasting life really sitting around sad wondering where to go and all the time it's right there for you to take"—"Supposin I dont want it"—"That's part of the picture where you say you dont want it, of course you want. . ."—"But I dont, I'm a creepy strange guy you dont even know"—("Cweepy? what's cweepy? Billie? what's cweepy?" is asking poor little Elliott)— And meanwhile Perry comes in for a minute and I pointblank say to him "I dont understand you Perry, I love you, dig you, you're wild, but what's all this business where you wanta kidnap little girls?" but suddenly as I'm asking that I see tears in his eyes and I realize he's in love with Billie and has always been, wow—I even say it, "You're in love with Billie aint ya? I'm sorry, I'm cuttin out"—"What are you talkin about man?"—It's a big argument then about how he and Billie are just friends so I start singing *Just Friends* like Sinatra "Two friends but not like before" but goodhearted Perry seeing me sing runs downstairs to get another bottle for me—But nevertheless the fish are dead and the chair is broken.

Perry in fact is a tragic young man with enormous potentials who's just let himself swing and float to hell I guess, unless something else happens to him soon, I look at him and realize that besides loving Billie secretly and truly he must also love old Cody as much as I do and all the world bettern I do yet he is the character who is always being put away behind bars for this—Rugged, covered with woe, he sits there with his black hair always over his brow, over his black eyes, his iron arms hanging helplessly like the arms of a powerful idiot in the madhouse, with the beauty of lostness pasted all over him—Who is he? in fact?—And why doesnt blonde Billie washing the homey dishes there acknowledge his love?—In fact me and Perry end up we're both sitting with hanging heads when Billie comes back in the livingroom and sees us like that, like two repentant catatonics in hell—Some Negro comes in and says if I give him a few dollars he'll get some pot but as soon as I give him five dollars he suddenly says "Well I aint gonna get nothin"—"You got five dollars, go out and get it"—"I aint sure I can get any"—I dont like him at all—I suddenly realize I can leap up and throw him on the floor and take the five dollars away from him but I dont even care about the money but I am mad about him doing that—"Who is that guy?"—I know that if I start fighting him he has a knife and we'll wreck Billie's livingroom too—But suddenly another Negro comes in and turns out a sweet visit talking about jazz and brotherhood and they all leave and me and Jacky are alone to wonder some more.

All the muscular gum of sex is such a bore, but Billie and I have such a fantastic sexball anyway that's why we're able to philosophize like that and agree and laugh together in sweet nakedness "Oh baby we're together crazy, we could live in an old log cabin in the hills and never say anything for years, it was meant that we'd meet"—She's saying all kinds of things as an idea begins to dawn on me: "Say I know Billie, let's leave the City and take Elliott with us and go to Monsanto's cabin in the woods for a week or two and forget everything"—"Yes I can call up my boss right now and get a coupla weeks off, Oh Jack let's do it"—"And it'll be good for Elliott, get away from all these sinister friends of yours, my God"—"Perry aint sinister."

    "We'll get married and go away and have a lodge in the Adirondacks, at night by the lamp we'll have simple suppers with Elliott"—"I'll make love to you always"—"But you wont even have to because we both realize we're bugs . . . our lodge will have truth written all over it but tho the whole world come smear it with big black paints of hate and lies we'll be falling dead drunk in truth"—"Have some coffee"—"My hands'll grow numb and I wont be able to handle the axe but still I'll be the truth man. . . I'll stand by the drape of the window night listening to the babble of all the world and I'll tell you about it"—"But Jack I love you and that's not the only reason why, dont you see that we're meant for each other from the beginning, didnt you see that when you came in with Cody and started calling me Julien for that silly reason you told me about where I look like some old buddy you know in New York"—"Who hates Cody's guts and Cody hates him"—"But dont you see what a waste it is?"—"But what about Cody? you want me to marry you but you love Cody and in fact Perry loves you too?"—"Sure but what's wrong with that or all that? there's perfect love between us forever there's no doubt about it but we only have two bodies"—(a strange statement)—I stand by the window looking out on the glittering San Francisco night with its magic cardboard houses saying "And you have Elliott who doesnt like me and I dont like him and in fact I dont like you and I dont like myself either, how about that?" (Billie says nothing to this but only stores up an anger that comes out later)—"But we can call Dave Wain and he'll drive us to Big Sur cabin and we'll be alone in the woods at least"—"I'm telling you that's what I wanta do!"—"Call him now!"—I tell her the number and she dials it like a secretary—"O the sad music of it all, I've done it all, seen it all, done everything with everybody" I say phone in hand, "the whole world's coming on like a high school sophomore eager to learn what he calls New things, mind you, the same old sing-song sad song truth of death . . . because the reason I yell death so much is because I'm really yelling life, because you cant have death without life, hello Dave? there you are? know what I'm callin you about? listen pal . . . take that big brunette Romana that Rumanian madwoman and pack her in Willie and come down to Billie's here and pick us up, we'll pack while you's en route, honey's on, and we'll all go spend two weeks of bliss in Monsanto's cabin"—"Does Monsanto agree?"—"I'll call him right now and ask him, he'll say sure"—"Well I thought I'd be painting Romana's wall tomorrow but maybe I'd a just got drunk doin that anyway: sure you wanta do all this now?"—"Yes yeh yeh, come on—" "And I can bring Romana?"—"Yes but why not?"—"And what's the purpose of all this?"—"Ah Daddy, maybe just to see you again and we can talk about purposes anywhere: you wanta go on a lecture tour to Utah university and Brown university and tell the well scrubbed kids?"—"Scrubbed with what?"—"Scrubbed with hopeless perfection of pioneer puritan hope that leaves nothing but dead pigeons to look at?"—"Okay I'll be right out . . . first I gotta get Willie's tank filled up and an oil change too"—"I'll pay you when you get here"—"I heard you were eloping with Billie"—"Who told you that?"—"It was in the paper today"—"Well we'll start off by getting into Willie again and dont bring Ron Blake, we'll be just two couples dig?"—"Yeh—and lissen I'll bring my surf castin rod and catch some fish down there"—"We'll have a ball—and listen Dave I'm grateful you're free and willing to drive us down there, I'm down in the mouth, I've been sitting here for a week drinking and the chair broke and the fish died and I'm all screwed up again"—"Well you shouldnt oughta drink that sweet stuff all the time and you never eat"—"But that's not the real trouble"—"Well we'll decide what the real trouble is"—"That's right"—"Methinks the real trouble is those pigeons"—"Why?"—"I dunno, remember when we were in East St. Louis with George, and Jack you said you'd love those beautiful dancing girls if you knew they would live forever as beautiful as they are?"—"But that's only a quote from Buddha"—"Yeh, but the girls didn't expect all that"—"How ya feeling Dave? what's Fagan doing tonight"—"Oh he's sitting in his room writing something, calls it his GOOFBOOK, has big wild drawings in it, and Lex Pascal is drunk again and the music is playing and I'm real sad and I'm glad you called"—"You like me Dave?"—"I aint got nothin else to do, kid"—"But you really have somethin else to do really?"—"Lissen never mind, I'll be up, you call Monsanto right away tho because we also gotta get the corral gate keys from him"— "I'm glad I know you Dave"—"Me too Jack"—"Why?"—"Maybe I wanted to stand on my head in the snow to prove it but I do, am glad, will be glad, after all that's right there's nothing else for us to do but solve these damn problems and I've got one right here in my pants for Romana"—"But that's so sick and tired to call life a problem that can be solved"—"Yes but I'm just repeating what I read in the dead pigeon textbooks"—"But Dave I love you"—"Okay I'll be right over."

32

WE PACK UP LITTLE Elliott's pathetic warmclothes and put food together and get the hamper all set and wait for Dave to come sadly in the night—And we have a big talk—"Billie but why did the fish die?" but she knows already they probably died because I gave them Kelloggs cornflakes or something went wrong, one thing sure is that she didnt forget to feed them or anything, it's all me, all my fault, I'd as soon be rusted by autumn too-much-think than be dead-fisher cause of those poor little hunks of golden death floating on that scummy water—It reminds me of the otter—But I cant explain it to Billie who's all abstract and talking about our abstract soul-meetings in hell, and little Elliott is pulling at her asking "Where we going? where we going? what for? what for?"—She's saying "And all because you think you dont deserve to be loved because you think you caused the death of the goldfish tho they probably just died on their own accord"—"Why would they do that? why? what kind of logic is that for fish to have?"—"Or because you think you drink too much and therefore every time you're feeling good on a little booze you give up and say your hands hang helpless, like you said last night when you were holding me with those hands blessing my heart and my body with your love, O Jack it's time for you to wake up and come with me or at least come with somebody and open your eyes to why God's put you here, stop all that staring at the floor, you and Perry both you're crazy—I'll draw you magic moon circles'll change all your luck"—I look her dead in the eye and it is blue and I say "O Billie, forgive me"—"But you see you go there talkin guilty again"—"Well I dont know all those big theories about how everything should be goddamit all I know is that I'm a helpless hunk of helpful horse manure looking in your eye saying Help me"—"But when you make those big final statements it doesnt help you"—"Of course I know that but what do you want?"—"I want us to get married and settle down to a sensible

understanding about eternal things"—"And you may be right"—I see
it all raving before me the endless yakking kitchen mouthings of life,
the long dark grave of tomby talks under midnight kitchen bulbs, in
fact it fills me with love to realize that life so avid and misunderstood
nevertheless reaches out skinny skeleton hand to me and to Billie
too—But you know what I mean.

And this is the way it begins.

33

IT SOUNDS ALL SO SAD but it was actually such a gay night as Dave and Romana came over and there's all the business of packing boxes and clothes down to the car, nipping out of bottles, getting ready in fact to sing all the way to Big Sur "Home On the Range" and "I'm Just a Lonsome Old Turd" by Dave Wain—Me sitting up front next to Dave and Romana for some reason maybe because I wanted to identify with my old broken front rockingchair and lean there flapping and singing but with Romana between us the seat is pinned down and no longer flaps—Meanwhile Billie is on the back mattress with sleeping child and off we go booming down Bay Shore to that other shore whatever it will bring, the way people always feel whenever they essay some trip long or short especially in the night—The eyes of hope looking over the glare of the hood into the maw with its white line feeding in straight as an arrow, the lighting of fresh cigarettes, the buckling to lean forward to the next adventure something that's been going on in America ever since the covered wagons clocked the deserts in three months flat—Billie doesnt mind that I dont sit in back with her because she knows I wanta sing and have a good time—Romana and I hit up fantastic medleys of popular and folk songs of all kinds and Dave contributes his New York Chicago blue light nightclub romantic baritone specialties—My wavering Sinatra is barely heard in fact—Beat on your knees and yell and sing Dixie and Banjo On My Knee, get raucous and moan out Red River Valley, "Where's my harmonica, I been meanin to buy me a eight dollar harmonica for eight years now."

It always starts out good like that, the bad moments—Nothing is gained or lost also by the fact that I insist we stop at Cody's en route so I can pick up some clothes I left there but secretly I want Evelyn to finally come face to face with Billie—It surprises me more however to see the look of absolute fright on Cody's face as we pour into his livingroom at midnight and I announce that Billie's in the jeep sleeping—Evelyn is not perturbed at all and in fact says to me privately in the kitchen "I guess it was bound to happen sometime she'd come here and see it but I guess it was destined to be you who'd bring her"—"What's Cody so worried about?"—"You're spoiling all his chance to be real secretive"—"He hasnt come and seen us for a whole week, that's in a way what happened, he just left me stranded there: I've been feeling awful, too"—"Well if you want you can ask her to come in"—"Well we're leaving in a minute anyway, you wanta see her at least?"—"I dont care"—Cody is sitting in the livingroom absolutely rigid, stiff, formal, with a big Irish stone in his eye: I know he's really mad at me this time tho I dont really know why—I go out and there's Billie alone in the car over sleeping Elliott biting her fingernail—"You wanta come in and meet Evelyn?"—"I shouldnt, she wont like that, is Cody there?"—"Yah"—So Willamine climbs out (I remember just then Evelyn telling me seriously that Cody always calls his women by their full first names, Rosemarie, Joanna, Evelyn, Willamine, he never gives them silly nicknames nor uses them).

The meeting is not eventful, of course, both girls keep their silence and hardly look at each other so it's all me and Dave Wain carrying on with the usual boloney and I see that Cody is really very sick and tired of me bringing gangs arbitrarily to his place, running off with his mistress, getting drunk and thrown out of family plays, hundred dollars or no hundred dollars he probably feels I'm just a fool now anyway and hopelessly lost forever but I dont realize that myself because I'm feeling good—I want us to resume down that road singing bawdier and darker songs till we're negotiating narrow mountain roads at the pitch of the greatest songs.

I try to ask Cody about Perry and all the other strange characters who visit Billie in the City but he just looks at me out of the corner eye and says "Ah, yah, hm,"—I dont know and I never will know what he's up to anyway in the long run: I realize I'm just a silly stranger goofing with other strangers for no reason far away from anything that ever mattered to me whatever that was—Always an ephemeral "visitor" to the Coast never really involved with anyone's lives there because I'm always ready to fly back across the country but not to any life of my own on the other end either, just a traveling stranger like Old Bull

Balloon, an exemplar of the loneliness of Doren Coit actually waiting
for the only real trip, to Venus, to the mountain of Mien Mo—Tho
when I look out of Cody's livingroom window just then I do see my
star still shining for me as it's done all these 38 years over crib, out
ship windows, jail windows, over sleepingbags only now it's dummier
and dimmer and getting blurreder damnit as tho even my own star
be now fading away from concern for me as I from concern for it—In
fact we're all strangers with strange eyes sitting in a midnight livingroom for nothing—And small talk at that, like Billie saying "I always
wanted a nice fireplace" and I'm yelling "Dont worry we got one at
the cabin hey Dave? and all the wood's chopped!" and Evelyn:-"What
does Monsanto think of you using his cabin all summer, weren't you
supposed to go there alone in secret?"—"It's too late now!" I sing swigging from the bottle without which I'd only drop with shame face flat
on the floor or on the gravel driveway—And Dave and Romana look
a little uneasy finally so we all get up to go, zoom, and that's the last
time I see Cody or Evelyn anyway.

And as I say our songs grow mightier as the road grows darker
and wilder, finally here we are on the canyon road the headlights just
reaching out there around bleak sand shoulders—Down to the creek
where I unlock the corral gate—Across the meadow and back to the
haunted cabin—Where on the strength of that night's booze and getaway gladness Billie and I actually have a good time lighting fires and
making coffee and *gong* to be together in the one sleepingbag easy as
pie after we've bundled up little Elliott and Dave and Romana have
retired in his double nylon bag by the creek in the moonlight.

No, it's the next day and night that concerns me.

34

THE WHOLE DAY BEGINS SIMPLY enough with me getting up feeling fair and going down to the creek to slurp up water in my palms and wash up, seeing the languid waving of one large brown thigh over the mass of Dave's nylons indicative of an early morning love scene, in fact Romana telling us later at breakfast "When I woke up this morning and saw all those trees and water and clouds I told Dave 'It's a beautiful universe we created'"—A real Adam and Eve waking up, in fact this being one of Dave's gladdest days because he'd really wanted to get away from the City again anyway and this time with a pretty doll, and's brought his surf casting gear planning a big day—And we've brought a lot of good food—The only trouble is there's no more wine so Dave and Romana go off in Willie to get some more anyway at a store 13 miles south down the highway—Billie and I are alone talking by the fire—I begin to feel extremely low as soon as last night's alcohol wears off.

Everything is trembly again, the trembling band, I cant for a fact even light the fire and Billie has to do it—"I cant light a fire any more!" I yell—"Well I can" she says in a rare instance when she lets me have it for being such a nut—Little Elliott is constantly pulling at her asking this and that, "What is that stick for, to put in the fire? why? how does it burn? why does it burn? where are we? when are we leaving" and the pattern develops where she begins to talk to him instead of me anyway because I'm just sitting there staring at the floor sighing—Later when he takes his nap we go down the path to the beach, about noon, both of us sad and silent—"What's the matter I wonder" I say out loud—She:-"Everything was alright last night when we slept in the bag together now you wont even hold my hand . . . goddamit I'm going to kill myself!"—Because I've begun to realize in my soberness that this thing has come too far, that I dont love Billie, that I'm leading her on, that I made a mistake dragging

everyone here, that I simply wanta go home now, I'm just plumb
sick and tired just like Cody I guess of the whole nervewracking
scene bad enough as it is always pivoting back to this poor haunted
canyon which again gives me the willies as we walk under the bridge
and come to those heartless breakers busting in on sand higher than
earth and looking like the heartlessness of wisdom—Besides I suddenly notice as if for the first time the awful way the leaves of the
canyon that have managed to be blown to the surf are all hesitantly
advancing in gusts of wind then finally plunging into the surf, to be
dispersed and belted and melted and taken off to sea—I turn around
and notice how the wind is just harrying them off trees and into the
sea, just hurrying them as it were to death—In my condition they
look human trembling to that brink—Hastening, hastening—In
that awful huge roar blast of autumn Sur wind.

   Boom, clap, the waves are still talking but now I'm sick and tired
of whatever they ever said or ever will say—Billie wants me to stroll
with her down towards the caves but I dont want to get up from
the sand where I'm sitting back to boulder—She goes alone—I suddenly remember James Joyce and stare at the waves realizing "All
summer you were sitting here writing the so called sound of the
waves not realizing how deadly serious our life and doom is, you
fool, you happy kid with a pencil, dont you realize you've been using
words as a happy game—all those marvelous skeptical things you
wrote about graves and sea death it's ALL TRUE YOU FOOL! Joyce
is dead! The sea took him! it will take YOU!" and I look down the
beach and there's Billie wading in the treacherous undertow, she's
already groaned several times earlier (seeing my indifference and
also of course the hopelessness at Cody's and the hopelessness of
her wrecked apartment and wretched life) "Someday I'm going to
commit suicide," I suddenly wonder if she's going to horrify the
heavens and me too with a sudden suicide walk into those awful
undertows—I see her sad blonde hair flying, the sad thin figure,
alone by the sea, the leaf-hastening sea, she suddenly reminds me
of something—I remember her musical sighs of death and I see the
words clearly imprinted in my mind over her figure in the sand:-ST.
CAROLYN BY THE SEA—"You were my last chance" she's said but

dont all women say that?—But can it be by "last chance" she doesnt
mean mere marriage but some profoundly sad realization of something in me she really needs to go on living, at least that impression
coming across anyway on the force of all the gloom we've shared—
Can it be I'm withholding from her something sacred just like she
says, or am I just a fool who'll never learn to have a decent eternally minded deepdown relation with a woman and keep throwing
that away for a song at a bottle?—In which case my own life is over
anyway and there are the Joycean waves with their blank mouths
saying "Yes that's so," and there are the leaves hurrying one by one
down the sand and dumping in—In fact the creek is freighting hundreds more of them a minute right direct from the back hills—That
big wind blasts and roars, it's all yellow sunny and blue fury everywhere—I see the rocks wobble as it seems God is really getting mad
for such a world and's about to destroy it: big cliffs wobbling in my
dumb eyes: God says "It's gone too far, you're all destroying everything one way or the other wobble boom the end is NOW."

"The Second Coming, tick tock," I think shuddering—St. Carolyn
by the Sea is going in further—I could run and go see her but she's so
far away—I realize that if that nut is going to try this I'll have to make
an awful run and swim to get her—I get up and edge over but just
then she turns around and starts back. . . "And if I call her 'that nut'
in my secret thoughts wonder what she calls me?"—O hell, I'm sick of
life—If I had any guts I'd drown myself in that tiresome water but that
wouldnt be getting it over at all, I can just see the big transformations
and plans jellying down there to curse us up in some other wretched
suffering form eternities of it—I guess that's what the kid feels—She
looks so sad down there wandering Ophelialike in bare feet among
thunders.

On top of that now here come the tourists, people from other cabins
in the canyon, it's the sunny season and they're out two three times
a week, what a dirty look I get from the elderly lady who's apparently
heard about the "author" who was secretly invited to Mr. Monsanto's
cabin but instead brought gangs and bottles and today worst of all
trollopes—(Because in fact earlier that morning Dave and Romana
have already made love on the sand in broad daylight visible not only

to others down the beach but from that high new cabin on the shoulder
of the cliff) (tho hidden from sight from the bridge by cliffwall)—So
it's all well known news now there's a ball going on in Mr. Monsanto's
cabin and him not even here—This elderly lady being accompanied by
children of all kinds—So that when Billie returns from the far end of
the beach and starts back with me down the path (and I'm silly with
a big footlong wizard pipe in my mouth trying to light it in the wind
to cover up) the lady gives her the once over real close but Billie only
smiles lightly like a little girl and chirps hello.

I feel like the most disgraceful and nay disreputable wretch on
earth, in fact my hair is blowing in beastly streaks across my stupid
and moronic face, the hangover has now worked paranoia into me
down to the last pitiable detail.

Back at the cabin I cant chop wood for fear I'll cut a foot off, I cant
sleep, I cant sit, I cant pace, I keep going to the creek to drink water
till finally I'm going down there a thousand times making Dave Wain
wonder as he's come back with more wine—We sit there slugging out
of our separate bottles, in my paranoia I begin to wonder why I get
to drink just the one bottle and he the other—But he's gay "I am now
going out surf castin and catch us a grabbag of fish for a marvelous
supper; Romana you get the salad ready and anything else you can
think of; we'll leave you alone now" he adds to gloomy me and Billie
thinking he's in our way, "and say, why dont we go to Nepenthe and
*priv*ate our grief tonight and enjoy the moonlight on the terrace with
Manhattans, or go see Henry Miller?"—"No!" I almost yell, "I mean
I'm so exhausted I dont wanta do anything or see anybody"—(already
feeling awful guilt about Henry Miller anyway, we've made an
appointment with him about a week ago and instead of showing up at
his friend's house in Santa Cruz at seven we're all drunk at ten calling
long distance and poor Henry just said "Well I'm sorry I dont get to
meet you Jack but I'm an old man and at ten o'clock it's time for me to
go to bed, you'd never make it here till after midnight now") (his voice
on the phone just like on his records, nasal, Brooklyn, goodguy voice,
and him disappointed in a way because he's gone to the trouble of
writing the preface to one of my books) (tho I suddenly now think in
my remorseful paranoias "Ah the hell with it he was only gettin in the

act like all these guys write prefaces so you dont even get to read the author first") (as an example of how really psychotically suspicious and loco I was getting).

Alone with Billie's even worse—"I cant see anything to do now," she says by the fire like an ancient Salem housewife ("Or Salem witch?" I'm leering)—"I could have Elliott taken care of in a private home or an orphanage and just go to a nunnery myself, there's a lot of them around—or I could kill myself and Elliott both"—"Dont talk like that"—"There's no other way to talk when there's no more directions to take"—"You've got me all wrong I wouldnt be any good for you"—"I know that now, you want to be a hermit you say but you dont do it much I noticed, you're just tired of life and wanta sleep, in a way that's how I feel too only I've got Elliott to worry about. . . I could take both our lives and solve that"—"You, creepy talk"—"You told me the first night you loved me, that I was most interesting, that you hadnt met anyone you liked so much then you just went on drinking, I really can see now what they say about you is true: and all the others like you: O I realize you're a writer and suffer through too much but you're really ratty sometimes . . . but even that I know you cant help and I know you're not really ratty but awfully broken up like you explained to me, the reasons . . . but you're always groaning about how sick you are, you really dont think about others enough and I KNOW you cant help it, it's a curious disease a lot of us have anyway only better hidden sometimes . . . but what you said the first night and even just now about me being St.Carolyn in the Sea, why dont you follow through with what your heart knows is Good and best and true, you give up so easy to discouragement . . . then I guess too you dont really want me and just wanta go home and resume your own life maybe with Louise your girlfriend"—"No I couldn't with her either, I'm just bound up inside like constipation, I cant move emotionally like you'd say emotionally as tho that was some big grand magic mystery everybody saying 'O how wonderful life is, how miraculous, God made this and God made that,' how do you know he doesnt hate what He did: He might even be drunk and not noticing what he went and done tho of course that's not true"—"Maybe God is dead"—"No, God cant be dead because He's the unborn"—"But you have all those philosophies and sutras you were talking about"—"But dont you see they've all become empty words, I realize I've been playing like a happy child with words words words in a big serious tragedy, look around"—"You could make some effort, damn it!"

But what's even ineffably worse is that the more she advises me and discussed the trouble the worse and worse it gets, it's as tho she didnt know what she was doing, like an unconscious witch, the more she tries to help the more I tremble almost too realizing she's doing it on purpose and knows she's witching me but it's all gotta be formally understood as "help" dingblast it—She must be some kind of chemical counterpart to me, I just cant stand her for a minute, I'm racked with guilt because all the evidence there seems to say she's a wonderful person sympathizing in her quiet sad musical voice with an obvious rogue nevertheless none of these rational guilts stick—All I feel is the invisible stab from her—She's hurting me!—At some points in our conversation I'm a veritable ham actor jumping up to twitch my head, that's the effect she has—"What's the matter?" she asks softly—Which makes me almost scream and I've never screamed in my life—It's the first time in my life I'm not confident I can hold myself together no matter what happens and be inly calm enough to even smile with condescension at the screaming hysterias of women in madwards—I'm in the same madward all of a sudden—And what's happened? what's caused it—"Are you driving me mad on purpose?" I finally blurt—But naturally she protests I'm talking out of my head, there's no such evident intention anywhere, we're just on a happy weekend in the country with friends, "Then there's something wrong with ME!" I yell— "That's obvious but why dont you try to calm down and for instance like make love to me, I've been begging you all day and all you do is groan and turn away as tho I was an ugly old bat"—She comes and offers herself to me softly and gently but I just stare at my quivering wrists—It's really very awful—It's hard to explain—Besides then the little boy is constantly coming at Billie when she kneels at my lap or sits on it or tries to soothe my hair and comfort me, he keeps saying in the same pitiful voice "Dont do it Billie dont do it Billie dont do it Billie" till finally she has to give up that sweet patience of hers where she answers his every little pathetic question and yell "Shut up! Elliott will you shut up! DO I have to beat you again!" and I groan "No!" but Elliott yells louder "Dont do it Billie dont do it Billie dont do it Billie!" so she sweeps him off and starts whacking him screamingly on the porch and I am about to throw in the towel and gasp up my last, it's horrible.

Besides when she beats Elliott she herself cries and then will be yelling madwoman things like "I'll kill both of us if you dont stop, you leave me no alternative! O my child!" suddenly picking him up and embracing him rocking tears, and gnashing of hair and all under those old peaceful bluejay trees where in fact the jays are still waiting for their food and watching all this—Even so Alf the Sacred Burro is in the yard waiting for somebody to give him an apple—I look up at the sun going down golden throughout the insane shivering canyon, that blasted rogue wind comes topping down trees a mile away with an advancing roar that when it hits the broken cries of mother and son in grief are blown away with all those crazy scattering leaves— The creek screeches—A door bangs horribly, a shutter follows suit, the house shakes—I'm beating my knees in the din and cant even hear that.

"What's I got to do with you committing suicide anyway?" I'm yelling—"Alright, it has nothing to do with you"—"So okay you have no husband but at least you've got little Elliott, he'll grow up and be okay, you can always meanwhile go on with your job, get married, move away, do something, maybe it's Cody but more than that I'd say it's all those mad characters making you insane and wanta kill yourself like that—Perry—"—"Dont talk about Perry, he's wonderful and sweet and I love him and he's much kinder to me than you'll ever be: at least he gives of himself"—"But what's all this giving of ourselves, what's there to give that'll help anybody"—"You'll never know you're so wrapped up in yourself"—We're now starting to insult each other which would be a healthy sign except she keeps breaking down and crying on my shoulder more or less again insisting I'm her last chance (which isnt true)—"Let's go to a monastery together," she adds madly—"Evelyn, I mean Billie you might go to a nunnery at that, by God get thee to a nunnery, you look like you'd make a nun, maybe that's what you need

all that talk about Cody about religion maybe all this worldly horror
is just holding you back from what you call your true realizing, you
could become a big reverend mother someday with not a worry on
your mind tho I met a reverend mother once who cried . . . ah it's all
so sad"—"What did she cry about?"—"I dont know, after talking to
me, I remember I said some silly thing like 'the universe is a woman
because it's round' but I think she cried because she was remembering
her early days when she had a romance with some soldier who died,
at least that's what they say, she was the greatest woman I ever saw,
big blue eyes, big smart woman . . . you could do that, get out of this
awful mess and leave it all behind"—"But I love love too much for
that"—"And not because you're sensual either you poor kid"—In fact
we quiet down a little and do actually make love in spite of Elliott
pulling at her "Billie dont do it dont do it Billie dont do it" till right in
the middle I'm yelling "Dont do what? what's he mean?—can it be he's
right and Billie you shouldnt do it? can it be we're sinning after all's
said and done? O this is insane!—but he's the most insane of them
all," in fact the child is up on bed with us tugging at her shoulder just
like a grownup jealous lover tryin to pull a woman off another man
(she being on top indication of exactly how helpless and busted down
I've become and here it is only 4 in the afternoon)—A little drama
going on in the cabin maybe a little different than what cabins are
intended for or the local neighbors are imagining.

35

BUT THERE'S AN AWFUL PARANOIAC element sometimes in orgasm that suddenly releases not sweet genteel sympathy but some token venom that splits up in the body—I feel a great ghastly hatred of myself and everything, the empty feeling far from being the usual relief is now as tho I've been robbed of my spinal power right down the middle on purpose by a great witching force—I feel evil forces gathering down all around me, from her, the kid, the very walls of the cabin, the trees, even the sudden thought of Dave Wain and Romana is evil, they're all coming now—I leave poor Billie face in hand and rush off to drink water in the creek but every time I do something like that I have to run back to be sorry and say so, but the moment I see her again "She's doing something else" I leer and I dont feel sorry at all—She's mumbling face in hands and the little boy's crying at her side—"My God she should get to a nunnery!" I think rushing back to the creek—Suddenly the water in the creek tastes different as tho somebody's thrown gasoline or kerosene in it upstream—"Maybe those neighbors wanta get back at me that's what!"—I taste the water carefully and I'm positive that's what happened.

Like an idiot I'm sitting by the creek staring when Dave Wain comes striding down with one fish on the line and his big cheerful western twang as tho nothing unusual's happened "Well boy I spent a whole two hours and look what I got! one measly but beautiful pathetic as you'll see holy little rainbow sea trout that I'm now going to clean—Now the way to clean fish is as follows," and he kneels innocently by the creek to show me how—I have nothing else to do but watch and smile—He says: "Be prepared to be taken on tour of Farollone Island within next two years, boy, with wild canaries actually lighting on your boat hundreds of miles out at sea—See I'm tryna to save money for a fishboat of my own, I think fishing is bettern anything and I intend to entirely reorganize my life for this tho I see the stern image of

Fagan shrieking with a Roshi stick, but you ought to see how fast you can bait up hundreds of herring and clean salmon in one and a half minutes, it's a fact, and you walk around in hickory shirts and wool knit caps—Man I know all about it and I'm writing a final definitive article on how clean hard work is the saviour of us all—When you're out there it's a very primal light, fishing is—You're a hunter—Birds find fish for you—Weather drives you—Foolish mind-hangs dissolve before utter fatigue and everything comes in"—As I squat there I imagine maybe Billie is telling Romana what happened in the cabin and Dave'll know in a while tho he seems to know a lot that's going on—He's hinted several times, like now, "You look like you're having the worse time of your life, that kid Elliott is enough to drive anybody crazy and Billie is sure a nervous little wench—Now here's the way you scale, with this here knife"—And I marvel that I cant be so useful and humanly simple and good enough to make small talk to make others feel better, like Dave, there he is long and hollow of cheeks from long drinking himself the past few weeks, but he's not complaining or moaning in the corner like me, at least he does something about it, he puts himself to the test—He gives me that feeling again that I'm the only person in the world who is devoid of human-beingness, damn it, that's true, that's the way I feel anyway—"Ah Dave someday you and me'll go fishing in your abandoned mining camp on the Rogue River, huh, we'll be feeling better by then somehow gaddamit"—"Well we've got to cut down on the sauce a whole lot, Jack," saying "Jack" sadly a lot like Jarry Wagner used to do on our Dharmabumming mountain climbs where we'd confide dolors, "yes, and we drink too many SWEET drinks in a way, you know all that sugar and no food is bound to upset your metabolism and fill your blood with sugar to the point where you aint got the strength of a hen; you especially you've been drinking nothin but sweet port and sweet Manhattans now for weeks—I promise you the holy flesh of this little fish will heal you," (chuckle).

I suddenly look at the fish and feel horrible all over again, that old death scheme is back only now I'm gonna put my big healthy Anglosaxon teeth into it and wrench away at the mournful flesh of a little living being that only an hour ago was swimming happily in the sea, in fact even Dave thinking this and saying: "Ah yes that little muzzling mouth was blindly sucking away in the glad waters of life and now look at it, here's where the fittin head's chopped off, you dont have to look, us big drunken sinners are now going to use it for our sacrificial supper so in fact when we cook it I'm going to say an Indian prayer for it hoping it's the same prayer the local Indians used—Jack in a way we might even start havin fun here and make a great week out of it!"—"Week?"—"I thought we was coming here for a week"—"Oh I said that didnt I . . . I feel awful about everything . . . I dont think I can make it. . . I'm going crazy with Billie and Elliott and me too . . . maybe I'll have to, maybe we'll have to leave or something, I think I'll die here"—And Dave is disappointed naturally and here I've already routed him up out of his own affairs to drive down here anyway, another matter to make me feel like a rat.

36

BUT DAVE'S MAKING THE BEST of clomping up and down the cabin pre-
paring the bag of cornmeal and starting the corn oil in the frying pan,
Romana too she's making an exquisite big salad with lots of mayon-
naise and in fact poor Billie is mutely helping her setting the table and
the little boy is crooning by the stove it's almost like a happy domes-
tic scene suddenly—Only I watch it from the porch with horrified
eyes—Also because their shadows in the lamplight gone casting on
the walls look huge and monsterlike and witch-like and warlock-like,
I'm alone in the woods with happy ghosts—The wind is howling as the
sun goes down so I go in, but I go out at once again madly to my creek,
always thinking the creek itself will give me water that will clear away
everything and reassure me forever (also remembering in my distress
Edgar Cayce's advice "Drink a lot of water") but "There's kerosene in
the water!" I yell in the wind, nobody hearing—I feel like kicking the
creek and screaming—I turn around and there's the cabin with its
warm interiors, the silent people inside all noticeably glum because
they cant understand anyway what's with the nut wandering in and
out from cabin to creek, silent, wan faced, stupefacted, trembling and
sweating like midsummer was on the roof and instead it's even cold
now—I sit in the chair with my back to the door and watch Dave as he
lectures on bravely.

  "What we're having is a sacrificial banquet with all kinds of goodies
you see laid in a regal spread around one little delicious fish so that
we all have to pray to the fish and take tiny little bites, we only have
about four bites apiece and there's all kinds of parts of the fish where
the bites are more significant—But beyond that the way to properly
fry a freshcaught fish is to be sure the oil is burning and furiously so
when you lay the fish in it, not burning but real hot oil, well yeh even
burning, hand me the spat, you then gently lay the fish into the oil
and create a tremendous crackling racket" (which he does as Romana

cheers) (and I glance at Billie and she's thinking of something else like a nun in the corner) but Dave keeps on making jokes till he actually has us all smiling—While the fish is cooking, tho, Romana as she's been doing all day is constantly handing me a bite to eat, some *hors d'oeuvres* or piece of tomato or other, apparently trying to help me feel better—"You've got to EAT" she and Dave keep saying but I dont want to eat and yet they're always holding out bites to my mouth until finally now I begin to frown thinking "What's all these bites they keep throwing at me, poison?—and what's wrong with my eyes, they're all dilated black like I've had drugs, all I've had is wine, did Dave put drugs in my wine or something? thinking it will help or something? or are they members of a secret society that dopes people secretly the idea being to enlighten them or something?" even as Romana is handing me a bite and I take it from her big brown hands and chew— She's wearing purple panties and purple bras, nothing else, just for fun, Dave's slappin her on the can joyfully as he cooks the supper, it's some big erotic natural thing to do for Romana, she believes in showing her beautiful big body anyway—In fact at one point when Billie's up leaning over a chair Dave goes behind Billie and playfully touches *her* and winks at me, but I'm not of all this like a moron and we could all be having fun such as soldiers dream the day away imagining, dammit—But the venoms in the blood are asexual as well as asocial and a-everything—"Billie's so nice and thin, like I'm used to Romana maybe I should switch around here for variety," says Dave at the sizzling frying pan—I look over my shoulder and see at first with a leap of joy but then with ominous fear an enormous full moon at full fat standing there between Mien Mo mountain and the north canyon wall, like saying to me as I look over my trembling shoulder "Hoo doo you."

But I say "Dave, look, as if all this wasnt enough" and I point out the moon to him, there's dead silence in the trees and also among us inside, there she is, vast lugubrious fullmoon that frights madmen and makes waters wave, she's got one or two treetops silhouetted and's got that whole side of the canyon lit up in silver—Dave just looks at the moon with his tired madness eyes (over-excited eyes, my mother'd said) and says nothing—I go out to the creek and drink water and come back and wonder about the moon and suddenly the four shadows in the cabin are all dead silent as tho they had conspired with the moon.

"Time to eat, Jack," says Dave coming out on the porch suddenly— No one's saying anything—I go in and sheepishly sit at the table like the useless pioneer who doesnt do anything to help the men or please the women, the idiot in the wagon train who nevertheless has to be fed—Dave stands there saying "Oh full moon, here is our little fish which we are now going to partake of to feed us so that we shall be stronger; thank you Fish people, thank you Fish god; thank you moon for making our light tonight; this is the night of the fullmoon fish which we now consecrate with the first delicate bite"—He takes his fork and opens the little fish carefully, it's beautifully breaded and fried and centered in a dazzle of salads and vegetables and cornmeal johnnycakes, he opens a funny gill, goes under, removes a strange bite and projects it to my mouth saying "Take the first bite Jack, just a little bite, and be sure to chew very slowly"—I do so, oily delicious bite but nothing delicious any more in my tongue—Then the others take their little holy bites, little Elliott's eyes shining with delight at this wonderful game that however has started to frighten me—For obvious reasons by now.

As we eat Dave announces that he and I are sick from too much drinking and by God we're going to reform and see to it that we shape up, then he launches into stories as usual, ending in a talkative ordinary supper that I think will sorta straighten me out at first but after supper I feel even worse, "That fish has all the death of otters and mouses and snakes right in it or something" I'm thinking—Billie is quietly washing the dishes with-out complaint, Dave is gladly smoking after-dinner cigarettes on the porch, but here I am again mooning by the creek hiding from all of them each five minutes tho I cant understand what makes me do it—I HAVE to get out of there—But I have no right to STAY AWAY—So I keep coming back but it's all an insane revolving automatic directionless circle of anxiety, back and forth, around and around, till they're really by now so perturbed by my increasing silent departures and creepy returns they're all sitting without a word by the stove but now their heads are together and they're whispering—From the woods I see those three shadowy heads whispering me by the stove—What's Dave saying?—And why do they look like they're plotting something further?—Can it be it was all arranged by Dave Wain via Cody that I would meet Billie and be driven mad and now they've got me alone in the woods and are going to give me final poisons tonight that will utterly remove all my control so that in the morning I'll have to go to a hospital forever and never write another line?—Dave Wain is jealous because I wrote 10 novels?—Billie has been assigned by Cody to get me to marry her so he'll get all my money? Romana is a member of the expert poisoning society (I've heard her mention tree spirits already, earlier in the car, and she's sung some strange songs the night before)—The three of them, Dave Wain in fact the chief conspirator because I know he does have amphetomine on his person and the needles in a little box, just one injection of a tomato, or of a portion of fish, or drops into a bottle of wine, and my eyes become mad wide and black like they are now, my nerves OO ouch, this is what I'm thinking—Still they sit there by the fire in dead silence, when I tromp into the cabin in fact they all start up again talking: sure sign—I walk out again, "I'm going down the road a ways"—"Okay"—But the moment I'm alone on the path a million waving moony arms are thrashing around me and every hole in the cliffs and burnt out trees I'd calmly passed a hundred times all summer in dead of fog, now has something moving in it quickly—I hurry back—Even on the porch I'm scared to see the familiar bushes near the outhouse or down by the broken treetrunk—And now a babble in the creek has somehow entered my head and with all the rhythm of the sea waves going "Kettle blomp you're up, you rop and dop, ligger lagger ligger" I grab my heat but it keeps babbling.

Masks explode before my eyes when I close them, when I look at the moon it waves, moves, when I look at my hands and feet they creep— Everything is moving, the porch is moving like ooze and mud, the chair trembles under me—"Sure you dont wanta go to Nepenthe for a Manhattan Jack?"—"No" ("Yeh and you'd dump poison in it" I think darkly but seriously hurt I could ever allow myself to think that about poor Dave)—And I realize the unbearable anguish of insanity: how uninformed people can be thinking insane people are "happy," O

God, in fact it was Irwin Garden once warned me not to think the
madhouses are full of "happy nuts," "There's a tightening around the
head that hurts, there's a terror of the mind that hurts even more,
they're so unhappy and especially because they cant explain it to anybody or reach out and be helped through all the hysterical paranoia
they are really suffering more than anyone in the world and I think in
the universe in fact," and Irwin knew this from observing his mother
Naomi who finally had to have a lobotomy—Which sets me thinking how nice to cut away therefore all that agony in my forehead and
STOP IT! STOP THAT BABBLING!—Because now the babbling's not
only in the creek, as I say it's left the creek and come in my head, it
would be alright for coherent babbling meaning something but it's
all brilliantly enlightened babble that does more than mean something: it's telling me to die because everything is over—Everything is
swarming all over me.

Dave and Romana retire again by the creek for a night's sweet sleep
under the moon while Billie and I sit there gloomy by the fire—Her
voice is crying: "It might make you feel better to just come in my
arms"—"I've got to try something, Billie after all I've told you I cant
make you see what's happening to me, you dont understand"—"Come
into our sleepingbag again like last night, just sleep"—We get in naked
but now I'm not drunk I'm aware of the real tight squeeze in there
and besides in my fever I'm perspiring so much it's unbearable, her
own skin is soaking wet from mine, yet our arms are outside in the
cold—"This won't do!"—"What'll you do?"—"Let's try the cot inside"
but maniacally I arrange the cot all screwy with a board on top of
it forgetting to put sleepingbag pads underneath like I'd done all
summer, I simply forget all that, Billie, poor Billie lies down with me
on this absurd board thinking I'm trying to drive my madness away
by self torturing ordeals—It's ridiculous, we lie there stiff as boards on
a board—I roll off and saying "We'll try something else"—I try laying
out the sleepingbag on the floor of the porch but the moment she's in
my arms a mosquito comes at me, or I burst out sweating, or I see a
flash of lightning, or I hear a big roaring Hymn in my head, or imagine a thousand people are coming down the creek talking, or the roar
of the wind is bringing flying treetrunks that will crush us—"Wait a

minute," I yell and get up to pace awhile and run down to drink water
by the creek where Dave and Romana are peacefully entangled—I
start cursing Dave "Bastard's got the only decent spot there is to sleep
in anyway, right there in that sand by the creek, if he wasnt here I
could sleep there and the creek would cover the noise in my head and
I could sleep there, with Billie even, all night, bastard's got my spot,"
and I kick back to the porch—Poor Billie's arms are outstretched to
me: "Please Jack, come on, love me, love me"—"I CANT"—"But why
cant you, if even we'll never see each other again let us our last night
be beautiful and something to remember forever."

     "Like a big ideal memory for both of us, cant you give me just
that?"—"I would if I could" I'm muttering around like a fussy old nut
inside the cabin looking for a match—I cant even light my cigarette,
something sinister blows it out, when it's lit it mortifies my hot mouth
anyway like a mouthful of death—I grab up another batch of bags
and blankets and start piling myself up on the other side of the porch
saying to Billie who's sighing now realizing it's hopeless "First I'll
try to take a nap by myself here then when I wake up I'll feel better
and come over to you"—So I try that, turning over rigidly my eyes
wide open staring full fright into the dark like the time in the movie
Humphrey Bogart who's just killed his partner trying to sleep by the
fire and you see his eyes staring into the fire rigid and insane—That's
just the way I'm staring—If I try to close my eyes some elastic pulls
them open again—If I try to turn over the whole universe turns over
with me but it's no better on the other side of the universe—I realize I may never come out of this and my mother is waiting for me
at home praying for me because she must know what's happening
tonight, I cry out to her to pray and help me—I remember my cat for
the first time in three hours and let out a yell that scares Billie—"All
right Jack?"—"Give me a little time"—But now she's started to sleep,
poor girl is exhausted, I realize she's going to abandon me to my fate
anyway and I cant help thinking she and Dave and Romana are all
secretly awake waiting for me to die—"For what reason?" I'm thinking
"this secret poisoning society, I know, it's because I'm a Catholic, it's
a big anti-Catholic scheme, it's Communists destroying everybody,
systematic individuals are poisoned till finally they'll have everybody,

this madness changes you completely and in the morning you no
longer have the same mind—the drug is invented by Airapatianz, it's
the brainwash drug, I always thought that Romana was a Communist
being a Rumanian, and as for Billie that gang of hers is strange, and
Cody dont care, and Dave's all evil just like I always figured maybe"
but soon my thoughts arent even as "rational" as that any more but
become hours of raving—There are forces whispering in my ear in
rapid long speeches advising and warning, suddenly other voices are
shouting, the trouble is all the voices are longwinded and talking very
fast like Cody at his fastest and like the creek so that I have to keep up
with the meaning tho I wanta bat it out of my ears—I keep waving at
my ears—I'm afraid to close my eyes for all the turmoiled universes
I see tilting and expanding suddenly exploding suddenly clawing in
to my center, faces, yelling mouths, long haired yellers, sudden evil
confidences, sudden rat-tat-tats of cerebral committees arguing about
"Jack" and talking about him as if he wasnt there—Aimless moments
when I'm waiting for more voices and suddenly the wind explodes
huge groans in the million treetop leaves that sound like the moon
gone mad—And the moon rising higher, brighter, shining down in
my eyes now like a streetlamp—The huddled shadowy sleeping figures
over there so coy—So human and safe, I'm crying "I'm not human any
more and I'll never be safe any more, Oh what I wouldnt give to be
home on Sunday afternoon yawning because I'm bored, Oh for that
again, it'll never come back again—Ma was right, it was all bound to
drive me mad, now it's done—What'll I say to her?—She'll be terrified
and go mad herself—*Oh ti Tykey, aide mué*—me who's just eaten fish
have no right to ask for brother Tyke again—"—An argot of sudden
screamed reports rattles through my head in a language I never heard
but understand immediately—For a moment I see blue Heaven and
the Virgin's white veil but suddenly a great evil blur like an ink spot
spreads over it, "The devil!—the devil's come after me tonight! tonight
is the night! that's what!"—But angels are laughing and having a big
barn dance in the rocks of the sea, nobody cares any more—Suddenly
as clear as anything I ever saw in my life, I see the Cross.

37

I SEE THE CROSS, it's silent, it stays a long time, my heart goes out to it, my whole body fades away to it, I hold out my arms to be taken away to it, by God I am being taken away my body starts dying and swooning out to the Cross standing in a luminous area of the darkness, I start to scream because I know I'm dying but I dont want to scare Billie or anybody with my death scream so I swallow the scream and just let myself go into death and the Cross: as soon as that happens I slowly sink back to life—Therefore the devils are back, commissioners are sending out orders in my ear to think anew, babbling secrets are hissed, suddenly I see the Cross again, this time smaller and far away but just as clear and I say through all the noise of the voices "I'm with you, Jesus, for always, thank you"—I lie there in cold sweat wondering what's come over me for years my Buddhist studies and pipesmoking assured meditations on emptiness and all of a sudden the Cross is manifested to me—My eyes fill with tears—"We'll all be saved—I wont even tell Dave Wain about it, I wont go wake him up down there and scare him, he'll know soon enough—now I can sleep."

I turn over but it's only begun—It's only one o'clock in the morning and the night wears on to the wheeling moon worse and worse till dawn by which time I've seen the Cross again and again but there's a battle somewhere and the devils keep coming back—I know if I could only sleep for an hour the whole complex of noisy brains would settle down, some control would come back somewhere inside there, some blessing would soothe the whole issue—But the bat comes silently flapping around me again, I see him clearly in the moonlight now his little head of darkness and wings that zigzag maddeningly so you cant even get a look at them—Suddenly I hear a hum, a definite flying saucer is hovering right over those trees where the hum must be, there are orders in there, "They're coming to get me O my God!"—I jump up and glare at the tree, I'm going to defend myself—The bat flaps in front of my face—"The bat is their representative in the canyon, his radar message they got, why dont they leave? doesnt Dave hear that awful hum?"—Billie is dead asleep but little Elliott suddenly thumps his foot, once—I realize he's not even asleep and knows everything that's going on—I lie down again and peek at him across the porch floor: I suddenly realizing he's staring at the moon and there he goes again, thumping his foot: he's sending messages—He's a warlock disguised as a little boy, he's also destroying Billie!—I get up to look at him feeling guilty too realizing this is all nonsense probably but he is not properly covered, his little bare arms are outside the blankets in the cold night, he hasnt even got a nightshirt, I curse at Billie—I cover him up and he whimpers—I go back and lie down with mad eyes looking deep inside me, suddenly a bliss comes over me as the sleep mechanism takes sinking hold—And there I am dreaming me and two kids are hired to work in the mountains on the same "ridge" as Desolation Peak (i.e. Mien Mo Mountain again) and start with a cliffside river crew who tell us two workers have apparently sunk in the cliffside snow and we must lean over sheer drops and see if we can "dump them out" or haul them in—All we do is lie there on crumbly snow a thousand foot fall to the river crumbling the snow off in slabs so big you wouldnt know if men were trapped in em or not—Not only that the bosses have special shoes on sliders that are holding them to the safe shore (like ski clamps) so I begin to realize they're only fooling us poor kids and we could have fallen too (I almost do)—(did)—(almost)—As observer of the story I see it's just an annual ritualistic joke to fool the new kids on the job who are then dispatched to the other side of the river to slump off *more* snow from sheer banks in hopes of finding the lost work-men—So we start there on a big trip, downriver first, but en route all the peasants tell us stories of the God Monster Machine on the other shore who makes sounds like certain birds and owls and has a million infernal contraptions enough to make you sick with all the slipshod windmill rickety details, as "Observer of the story" again I see it's just a trick to make us scared when we get there at night and hear actual natural sounds of birds, owls, etc. thinking as green rookies in the country it's that "Monster"—Meanwhile we sign on to go to the main mountain but I promise myself if I dont like the work there I'll come back get my old job on Desolation—Already our employers have shown a murderous sense of humor—I arrive at Mien Mo Mountain which is like Raton Canyon again but has a large tho dry rot river running in the wide hole and down there on many rocks are huge brooding vultures—Old bums row out to them and pull them clumsily off the rocks and start feeding them like pets, bites of red meat or red mite, tho at first I thought the eccentric old town bums wanted them to eat or to sell (still maybe so) because before I study this I look and see hundreds of slowly fornicating vulture couples on the town dump—These are now humanly formed vultures with human shaped arms, legs, heads, torsos, but they have rainbow colored feathers, and the men are all quietly sitting *behind* Vulture Women slowly somehow fornicating at them in all the same slow obscene movement—Both man and woman sit facing the same direction and somehow there's contact because you can see all their feathery rainbow behinds slowly dully monotonously fornicating on the dumpslopes—As I pass I even see the expression on the face of a youngish blond vulture man eternally displeased because his Vulture Mistress is an old Yakker who's been arguing with him all the time—His face is completely human but inhumanly pasty like uncooked pale pie dough with dull seamed buggy horror that he's doomed to all this enough to make me shudder in sympathy, I even see her awful expression of middle-aged pie dough tormentism—They're so human!—But suddenly me and the two kid workers are taken to the Vulture People respectable quarter of town to our apartment where a Vulture Woman and her daughter show us our rooms—Their faces are leprous thick with softy yeast but pamted with makeup to make them like thick Christmas dolls and dull and fuzzy but human expressions, like with thick lips of rubber muzz, fat expressions all crumbly like cracker meal, yellow pizza puke faces, disgusting us tho we say nothing—The apartment has dirty beatnik beds and mattresses everywhere but I walk thru the back looking for a sink—It's *huge*—An endless walk thru long greasy pantries and vast washrooms a block long with single filthy little sink all dark and slimey like underground Lowell High School crumbling basements—Finally I come to the Kitchen where we "new workers" are s'posed to cook little meals all summer—It's vast stone

fireplaces and stone stoves all rancid and greasy from a month-old
Vulture People Banquet Orgy with still dozens of uncooked chickens lying around on the floor, among garbage and bottles—Rancid
stale grease everywhere, nobody's ever cleaned it up or knew how and
the place as big as a garage—I push my way out of there pushing a
huge greasystink foodstained tray of some sort hurrying away from
the big stinky emptiness and horror—The fat golden chickens lie
rotten upsidedown on littered stone slabs—I hurry out never having
seen such a dirty sight in my life. Meanwhile I learn the two boys are
studying a hamper full of Vulture Food for us and one of them wisely
says "Blisters in our sugar," meaning the Vultures put their blisters
in our sugar so we'll "die" but instead of being really dead we'll be
taken to the Underground Slimes to walk neck deep in steaming
mucks pulling huge groaning wheels (among small forked snakes)
so the devil with the long ears can mine his Purple Magenta Square
Stone that is the secret of all this Kingdom—You end up down there
groaning and pulling thru dead bodies of other people even your own
family floating in the ooze—If you succeed you can become a pasty
Vulture Person obscenely fornicating slowly on the dump above, I
think, either that or the devil just invents the Vulture People with
what's left over out of the underground Hell—"Beans anyone?" I hear
myself saying as *thump*! I'm awake again! Elliott has thumped his foot
just at that moment on the porch!—I look over there!—He's doing it
on purpose, he knows everything that's going on!—What on earth
have I brought these people for and why just this particular night of
that moon that moon that moon?

I'm up again and pacing up and down and drinking water at the
creek, Dave and Romana's lump figures in the moonlight dont move,
like hypocrites, "Bastard has my only sleeping spot"—I clutch my
head, I'm so alone in all this—I go fearfully casting about for control
back inside the cabin by the lighted lamp, a smoke, trying to squeeze
the last red drop out of the rancid port bottle, no go—Now that Billie's
asleep and so still and peaceful I wonder if I can sleep just by lying
beside her and holding her—I do just this, crawling in with all my
clothes which I've put on because I'm afraid of going mad naked
or of not being able to suddenly run away from everything, in my

shoes, she moans a little in her sleep and resumes sleeping as I hold her with those rigid staring eyes—Her blonde flesh in the moonlight, the poor blonde hair so carefully washed and combed, the ladylike little body also a burden to carry around like my own but so frail, thinnish, I just stare at her shoulders with tears—I'd wake her up and confess everything but I'll only scare her—I've done irreparable harm ("Garradarable narm!" yells the creek)—All my self sayings suddenly blurting babbles so the meaning cant even stay a minute I mean a moment to satisfy my rational endeavors to hold control, every thought I have is smashed to a million pieces by millionpieced mental explosions that I remember I thought were so wonderful when I'd first seen them on Peotl and Mescaline, I'd said then (when still innocently playing with words) "Ah, the manifestation of multiplicity, you can actually see it, it aint just words" but now it's "Ah the kese-lamaroyot you rot"—Till when dawn finally comes my mind is just a series of explosions that get louder and more "multiply" broken in pieces some of them big orchestral and then rainbow explosions of sound and sight mixed.

At dawn also I've almost dimmed into sleep three times but I swear (and this is something I remember that makes me realize I dont understand what happened at Big Sur even now) the little boy some-how thumped his foot just at the moment of drowse, to instantly wake me up, wide awake, back to my horror which when all is said and done is the horror of all the worlds the showing of it to me being damn well what I deserve anyway with my previous blithe yakkings about the sufferings of others in books.

Books, shmooks, this sickness has got me wishing if I can ever get out of this I'll gladly become a millworker and shut my big mouth.

38

DAWN IS MOST HORRIBLE of all with the owls suddenly calling back
and forth in the misty moon haunt—And even worse than dawn is
morning, the bright sun only GLARING in on my pain, making it
all brighter, hotter, more maddening, more nervewracking—I even
go roaming up and down the valley in the bright Sunday morning
sunshine with bag under arm looking hopelessly for some spot to
sleep in—As soon as I find a spot of grass by the path I realize I cant
lie down there because the tourists might walk by and see me—As
soon as I find a glade near the creek I realize it's too sinister there, like
Hemingway's darker part of the swamp where "the fishing would be
more tragic" somehow—All the haunts and glades having certain special evil forces concentrated there and driving me away—So haunted
I go wandering up and down the canyon crying with that bag under
my arm: "What on earth's happened to me? and how can earth be like
that?"

Am I not a human being and have done my best as well as anybody else? never really trying to hurt anybody or half-hearted cursing Heaven?—The words I'd studied all my life have suddenly gotten
to me in all their serious and definite deathliness, never more I be a
"happy poet" "Singing" "about death" and allied romantic matters,
"Go thou crumb of dust you with your silt of a billion years, here's
a billion pieces of silt for you, shake that out of your shaker"—And
all the green nature of the canyon now waving in the morning sun
looking like a cruel idiot convocation.

Coming back to the sleepers and staring at them wild eyed like my
brother'd once stared at me in the dark over my crib, staring at them
not only enviously but lonely inhuman isolation from their simple
sleeping minds—"But they all look dead!" I'm carking in my canyon,
"Sleep is death, everything is death!"

The horrible climax coming when the others finally get up and pook

about making a troubled breakfast, and I've told Dave I cant possibly
stay here another minute, he must drive us all back to town, "Okay but
I sure wish we could stay a week like Romana wants to do,"—"Well
you drive me and come back"—"Well I dunno if Monsanta would like
that we've already dirtied up the place aplenty, in fact we've got to dig
a garbage pit and get rid of the junk"—Billie offers to dig the garbage
pit but does so by digging a neat tiny coffinshaped grave instead of
just a garbage hole—Even Dave Wain blinks to see it—It's exactly the
size fit for putting a little dead Elliott in it, Dave is thinking the same
thing I am I can tell by a glance he gives me—We've all read Freud suf-
ficiently to understand something there—Besides little Elliott's been
crying all morning and has had two beatings both of them ending up
crying and Billie saying she cant stand it any more she's going to kill
herself—

    And Romana too notices it, the perfect 4 foot by 3 foot neatly sided
grave like you're ready to sink a little box in it—Horrifying me so
much I take the shovel and go down to dump junk into it and mess
up the neat pattern somehow but little Elliott starts screaming and
grabs the shovel and refuses I go near the hole—So Billie herself goes
and starts filling the garbage in but then looks at me significantly (I'm
sure sometimes she really did aspire to make me crazy) "Do you want
to finish the job yourself?"—"What do you mean?"—"Cover the earth
on, do the honors?"—"What do you mean do the honors!"—"Well I
said I'd dig the garbage pit and I've done that, aint you supposed to
do the rest?"—Dave Wain is watching fascinated, there's something
screwy he sees there too, something cold and frightening—"Well
okay" I say, "I'll dump the earth over it and tamp it down" but I go
down to do this Elliott is screaming "NO no no no no!" ("My God, the
fishes' bones are in that grave" I realize too)—"What's the matter he
wont let me go near that hole! why did you make it look like a grave?"
I finally yell—But Billie is only smiling quietly and steadily at me,
over the grave, shovel in hand, the kid weeping tugging the shovel,
rushing up to block my way, trying to shove me back with his little
hands—I cant understand any of it—He's screaming as I grab the
shovel as tho I'm about to bury Billie in there or something or himself
maybe—"What's the matter with this kid is he a cretin?" I yell.

With the same quiet steady smile Billie says "Oh you're so fucking neurotic!"

I simply get mad and dump earth over the garbage and tromp it all down and say "The hell with all this madness!"

I get mad and stomp up on the porch and throw myself in the canvas chair and close my eyes—Dave Wain says he's going down the road to investigate the canyon a bit and when he comes back the girls will have finished packing and we'll all leave—Dave goes off, the girls clean up and sweep, the little kid is sleeping and suddenly hopelessly and completely finished I sit there in the hot sun and close my eyes: and there's the golden swarming peace of Heaven in my eyelids—It comes with a sure hand a soft blessing as big as it is beneficent, i.e., endless—I've fallen asleep.

I've fallen asleep in a strange way, with my hands clasped behind my head thinking I'm just going to sit there and think, but I'm sleeping like that, and when I wake up just one short minute later I realize the two girls are both sitting behind me in absolute silence—When I'd sat down they were sweeping, but now they were squatting behind my back, facing each other, not a word—I turn and see them there— Blessed relief has come to me from just that minute—Everything has washed away—I'm perfectly normal again—Dave Wain is down the road looking at fields and flowers—I'm sitting smiling in the sun, the birds sing again, all's well again.

I still cant understand it.

Most of all I cant understand the miraculousness of the silence of the girls and the sleeping boy and the silence of Dave Wain in the fields—Just a golden wash of goodness has spread over all and over all my body and mind—All the dark torture is a memory—I know now I can get out of there, we'll drive back to the City, I'll take Billie home, I'll say goodbye to her properly, she wont commit no suicide or do anything wrong, she'll forget me, her life'll go on, Romana's life will go on, old Dave will manage somehow, I'll forgive them and explain everything (as I'm doing now)—And Cody, and George Baso, and ravened McLear and perfect starry Fagan, they'll all pass through one way or the other—I'll stay with Monsanto at his home a few days and he'll smile and show me how to be happy awhile, we'll drink dry wine instead of sweet and have quiet evenings in his home—Arthur Ma will come to quietly draw pictures at my side—Monsanto will say "That's all there is to it, take it easy, everything's okay, dont take things too serious, it's bad enough as it is without you going the deep end over imaginary conceptions just like you always said yourself"—I'll get my ticket and say goodbye on a flower day and leave all San Francisco behind and go back home across autumn America and it'll all be like it was in the beginning—Simple golden eternity blessing all— Nothing ever happened—Not even this—St. Carolyn by the Sea will go on being golden one way or the other—The little boy will grow up and be a great man—There'll be farewells and smiles—My mother'll be waiting for me glad—The corner of the yard where Tyke is buried will be a new and fragrant shrine making my home more homelike somehow—On soft Spring nights I'll stand in the yard under the stars—Something good will come out of all things yet—And it will be golden and eternal just like that—There's no need to say another word.

"SEA"
Sounds of the Pacific Ocean at Big Sur

"SEA"
Cherson!
Cherson!
You aint just whistlin
Dixie, Sea—
Cherson! Cherson!
We calcimine fathers
here below!
Kitchen lights on—
Sea Engines from Russia
seabirding here below—
When rocks outsea froth
I'll know Hawaii
cracked up & scramble
up my doublelegged cliff
to the silt of
a million years—
Shoo—Shaw—Shirsh—
Go on die salt light
You billion yeared
rock knocker
Gavroom
Seabird
Gabroobird
Sad as wife & hill
Loved as mother & fog
Oh! Oh! Oh!
Sea! Osh!
Where's yr little Neppytune
tonight?

These gentle tree pulp pages
which've nothing to do
with yr crash roar,
liar sea, ah,
were made for rock

tumble seabird digdown
footstep hollow weed
move bedarvaling
crash? Ah again?
Wine is salt here?
Tidal wave kitchen?
Engines of Russia
in yr soft talk—

Les poissons de la mer
parle Breton—
Mon nom es Lebris
de Keroack—
Parle, Poissons, Loti,
parle—
Parlning Ocean sanding
crash the billion rocks—
Ker plotsch—

Shore—shoe—
god—brash—
The headland looks like
a longnosed Collie sleeping
with his light on his
nose, as the ocean,
obeying its accomodations
of mind, crashes in
rhythm which could
& will intrude, in thy
rhythm of sand
thought—
—Big frigging shoulders
on *that* sonofabitch

Parle, O, parle, mer, parle,
Sea speak to me, speak
to me, your silver you light
Where hole opened up in Alaska
Gray—shh—wind in
The canyon wind in the rain
Wind in the rolling rash
Moving and t wedel
Sea
sea
Diving sea
O bird—la vengeance
De la roche
Cossez
Ah

Rare, he rammed the gate
rare over by Cherson, Cherson,
we calcify fathers here below

—a watery cross, with weeds
entwined—This grins restoredly,
low sleep—Wave—Oh, no,
shush—Shirk—Boom plop
Neptune now his arms extends
while one millions of souls
sit lit in caves of darkness
—What old bark? The dog
mountain? Down by the Sea
Engines? God rush—Shore—
Shaw—Shoo—Oh soft sigh
we wait hair twined like
larks—Pissit—Rest not
—Plottit, bisp tesh, cashes,
re tav, plo, aravow,
shirsh,—Who's whispering over
there—the silly earthen creek!
The fog thunders—We put

silver light on face—We
took the heroes in—A billion
years aint nothing—

O the cities here below!
The men with a thousand
arms! the stanchions of
their upward gaze! the
coral of their poetry! the
sea dragons tenderized, meat
for fleshy fish—
Navark, navark, the fishes
of the Sea speak Breton—
wash as soft as people's
dreams—We got peoples
in & out the shore, they call
it shore, sea call it
pish rip plosh—The
5 billion years since
earth we saw substantial
chan—Chinese are
the waves—the woods
are dreaming

No human words bespeak
the token sorrow older
than old this wave
becrashing smarts the
sand with plosh
of twirléd sandy
thought—Ah change
the world? Ah set
the fee? Are rope the
angels in all the sea?
Ah ropey otter
barnacle'd be—
Ah cave, Ah crosh!
A feathery sea

Too much short—Where
Miss Nop tonight?
Wroten Kerarc'h
in the labidalian
aristotelian park
with slime a middle
—And Ranti forner
who pulled pearls by
rope to throne
the King by
the roll in the
forest of everseas?
Not everseas, *be* seas
—Creep
Crash
The woman with her body
in the sea—The frog who
never moves & thunders, sharsh
—The snake with his body
under the sand—The dog
with the light on his nose,
supine, with shoulders so
enormous they reach back to
rain crack—The leaves hasten
to the sea—We let them
hasten to be wetted & give
em that old salt change, a
nuder think will make you see
they originate from the We Sea
anyway—No dooming booms
on Sunday afternoons—We
run thru the core of cliffs,

blam up caves, disengage no
jelly or jellied pendant
thinkers—

Our armies of

anchored seaweed in the
coves give of the smell
of jellied salt—
Reach, reach, some leaves
havent hastened near
enuf—Roll, roll, purl
the sand shark floor
a greeny pali andarva
—Ah back—Ah forth—
Ah shish—Boom, away,
doom, a day—Vein we

firm—The sea is We—
Parle, parle, boom the
earth—Arree—Shaw,
Sho, Shoosh, flut,
ravad, tapavada pow,
coof, loof, roof,—
No,no,no,no,no,no—
Oh ya, ya, ya, yo, yair—
Shhh—

Which one? the one? Which
one? The one ploshed—
The ploshed one? the same,
ah boom—Who's that ant
that giant golden saltchange
ant magnifying my mountain
of feet? 'Tis Finder, finding
the change in thought to join
the boomer hangers in the
cave a light—And built a
house above it? Never fear,
naver foir, les bretons qui
parlent la langue de la Mar
sont español comme le cul
du Kurd qui dit le maha
prajna paramita du Sud?

Ah oui! Ke Vlum!
Glum sea, silent me—

They aint about to try
it them ants who wear
out tunnels in a week
the tunnel a million years
won—no—Down around
the headland slobs for weed,
the chicken of the sea
go yak! they sleep—
Aroar, aroar, arah, aroo—
Otter me otter me daughter me sea
—me last blue lagoon inside of
me, the sea—Divine is the
substance all over the Sea—
Of space we speak &
hasten—Let no mouth
swallow the sea—Gavril—
Gavro—the Cherson Chinese
& Old Fingernail sea—Is
ringin yr ear? Dier, dee?
Is Virgin you trying to
fathom me

Tiresome old sea, aint you sick
& tired of all of this merde?
this incessant boom boom
& sand walk—you people
hoary rockies here to Fuegie
& never get sad? Or despair

like a German phoney?
Just gloom booboom & green
on foggy nights—the fog is part
of us—
I know, but tired
as I can be listening to all
this silly majesty—

Bashô!
Lao!
Pop!
Who is this fish
sitting unsunk? Run up
a Hawaii typhoon smash him
against his rock—We'll jelly you,
jellied man, show you essential
jello of the sea—King
of the Sea.

No Monarc'h ever Irish be?
Ju see the Irish sea?
Green winds on tamarack vines—
Joyce—James—Shhish—
Sea—Sssssss—see
—Varash
—mnavash la vache
écriture—the sea dont say
muc'h actually—

Gosh, she,
huzzy, tow, led men
on, Ulysses and all them
fair headed moin—
Terplash, & what difference

make! One little white
spark of light!
Hair woven hands
Penelope seaboat
smeller—Courtiers in
Telemachus 'sguise
dropedary dropedary
creep—Or—
Franc gold rippled
that undersea creek
where fish fish for
fisher men—Salteen

breen the wet Souwesters
of old Portugee Prayers
Tsall tangled, changed,
salt & drop the sand

& weed & water brains
entangled—Rats
of old Venetian yellers
Ariel Calibanned
to Roma Port—
Pow—spell—
Speak you parler,
in this my mother's
parlor, wash your
undershoes when you
come in, say thanks
to foggy moon

Go brash, Topahta
offat,—we'll gray
ye rose—Morning
primord creeper sees
the bird of paravision

dying tweet the yellow
mouthroof! How sweet
the earth, yells sand!
Xcept when tumble
boom!
O we wait too
for Heaven—all
in One—
All is there
in fair & sight

I'm going to wash now
old Pavia down,
& pack my salt
to Either Town—

Cliffs of Antique
aint got no rose,
the morning's seen
the ledder pose—

Boom de boom dey
the sea is me—
We are the sea—
It aint all snow

We wash Fujiyama down
soon, & sand
crookbird back—
We hie bash
rock—ak—
Long short—
Low and easy—
Wind & many freezing
bottoms on luckrock—
Rappaport—
Endymion thou tangled
dreamer love my thigh
—Rose, Of Shelley,
Rose, O Urns!
Ogled urns in fish eye

Cinco sea the Chico sea
the Magellan headland sea
—What hype sidereal did he put down
bending beatnik sea goatee
over old goat manuscripts
to find the other side of Flat?
See round, see the end of me?
Rounden huge bedoom?
Awp hole cave & shwrul—
sand & salt & hair eyes
—Strong enuf to make
coffee grow in your hair—

Whose plantation Neptune got?
That of Atlas still down there,
Hesperid's his feet, Sur his sleet,
Irish Sea fingertip
& Cornwall aye his soul
bedoom

Shurning—Shurning—plop
be dosh—This sigh old learning's
high beside me—Rough
old hands have played out
pedigree, we've sunk more boats
than dreamer'll ever ever see
—Burning—Burning—The world
is burning & needs waaater
—I'll have a daughter,
oughter, wait & seee—
Churning, Churning, Me—
Panties—Panties—
these ancient fancies are
so girling—You've not seen
mermaids in my actual sea
—You've not seen sexless babies
with breasts of Majesty—
My wife—My wife—
Her name is Oh so really
high life

The low life Kingdom where
we part out tea, is sea
side Me—
Josh—coof—patra—
Aye ee mo powsh—
Ssst—Cum here read me—
Dirty postcard—Urchin sea—
Karash your name—?
Wanta swim, sink or swim?
Ears ringing again?

Sea vibrate rhythm
crash sets off cave
hanger blowers whistling
dog ear back—to sea—
Arree—
Gerudge Napoleon nada—
Nada

Pluto eats the sea—
Room—
Hands folded by the sea—
"On est toutes cachez, mange
le silence," dit les poissons de la
mer—Ah Mar—Gott—
Thalatta—Merde—Marde
de mer—Mu mer—Mak a vash—
The ocean is the mother—
Je ne suis pas mauvaise quand j'sui
tranquil—dans les tempêtes
j'cri! Come une folle!
j'mange, j'arrache toutes!
Clock—Clack—Milk—

Mai! mai! mai! ma!
says the wind blowing sand—
Pluto eats the sea—
Ami go—da—che pop
Go—Come—Cark—
Care—Kee ter da vo
Kataketa pow! Kek kek kek!
Kwakiutl! Kik!
Some of theserather taratasters
trapped hyra tchere thaped
the anadondak ram ma lat
round by Krul to Pat the lat
rat the anaakakalked
romon tottek
Kara VOOOM

frup—
Feet cold? wade—Mind sore?
sim—sin—Horny?—lay the sea?
Corny? try me—
Ussens here hang no more
here we go, ka va ra ta
plowsh, shhh,
and more, again, ke vlook
ke bloom & here comes
big Mister Trosh
—more waves coming,
every syllable windy

Back wash palaver
paralarle—paralleling
parle pe Saviour

A troublesome spirit
hanging here cant make it
in the void—The sea'll
only drown me—These words
are affectations
of sick mortality—
We try to make our way
in self reliance, aid
not ever comes too quick
from wherever & whatever
heaven dear may have
suggested to promise us—

But these waves scare me—
I am going to die
in full despair—

Wake up where?
On second breath in life
the atmosphere is dearer
maybe closer to Heaven
—O Paradise—

Is the sea really so bad?
Have you sent men
here for this cold clown
& monstrous eater at the
world? whose sound
I mock?

God I've got to believe in you
or live in death!
Will you save us—all?
Soon or now?
Send illumination
to our drowning brains
—We're pitiful, Lord,
we need yr help!
Save us, Dear—
(Save yourself, God man,
ha ha!)
If you were God man
you'd command these waves
to very well Tennyson stop
& even Tennyson
is dear
now dead
Leave it to the light
Concern yourself with supper,
& an eye

somebody's eye—a wife,

 a girl, a friend, an animal
—a blood let drop—
he for his sea,
he for his fire,
thee for thy desire

"The sea drove me away
& yelled 'Go to your desire!'
—As I hurried up the valley

It added one last yell:-
'And laugh!'"

Even the sea cant stop me from
writing something to read in my old age
—This is the chart of brief forms,
this sea the briefest—Shish yourself—
After scaring me like that, Mar,
I'll excoriate yr slum—yr
iodine weeds & slime hoops,
even yr dried hollow seaweed
stinks—you stink all over—
Boom—Try that, creep—
The little Monterey fishingboat
glides downward home 15 miles to go,
be home to fried fish & beer b'five—
It guides the sea its bird routes—
—Silver loss forever outward
—From blue sky of human bridges
to the massive mawkcloud sea center
heap—to the gray—
Some boys call it gunboat blue,
or gray, but I call it
the Civil War of Rocks
—Rocks 'come air, rocks 'come water,
& rock rocks—
Kara tavira, mnash grand bash
—poosh l'abas—croosh
L'a haut—Plash au pied—
Peeeee—Rolle test boulles—
Manche d'la rache—
The handsome King prevails
over boom sing bird head—
"Crache tes idées," spit yr ideas,
says the sea, to me, quite
appro priate ly—
Pss! pss! pss!
Ps! girl inside!

Red shoes scum, eyes of old
sorcerers, toenails hanging down
in the barrel of old firkin cheese
the Dutchman forgot t'eat that
tempest

nineteen O
sixteen—
When torpedoed by gunboat
Pedro in the Valley
of a Million Fees?

When Magellan crosseyed
ate the Amazonian feet—
And, Ah, when Colombo cross't!
When Drake sir francised the waves
with feeding of the blue jay
dark—pounded his aleward
tank before the boom,
housed up all thoughts of Erik
the Red the Greenland caperer
& builder of rockdungs in New
Port—*New*—yet—
Oldport Indian Fishhead—
Oldport Tattoo Kwakiutl Headpost
taboo potash Coyotl potlatch?
Old Primitive Columbia.—
Named for Colom *bus*?
Name for Aruggio Vesmarica—
Ar!—Or!—Da!
What about Verrazano?
he sailed!—
He Verrazano zailed & we
statened his Island in on deep
in on dashun—

Rotted the Wallower?
Sinners liars goodmen all
sink waterswim drink Neptune's

nectar the zal sotat—
Zal sotate name for crota?
Crota ta crotte, you aint
'bout to find (Jesus Christian!)
any dry turds here below—
Why fo no?
Go crash yonder rock
of bleak with yr filet mignon teeth
& see—For you, the hearth,
the heart, the lock of hair—

For me, for us, the Sea,
the murdering of time by eating
lusty cracks of lip feed wave
at aeons of sandy artistry
till nothing's left but old age
newmorning primordial pain
of sitters by
the unborn
bird
of roses yet undone—

With weeds your roses,
sand crabs your hummers?
With buzzers in the sea!
With runners in the deep!

This Sceptred Osh, this wide leg
spanning rock U.S. to rock
Ja Pan, this onstable
roller roaming all,
this ploosher at yr gory
dry dung door, this mouth
of silverwhite arring to hold thee,
this purger of conscience
arra for thee—
No mouse in here but's got
a little glee—and
aft, or oft, the osprey

in his glee's agley—
Oh purty purty ocean
me—
Sop! bring the Scepter down!
Again you've accepted me!

Breathe our iodine, filthy yr drink,
faint at feet wet, drop
yr profile move it in the sea,
float weeded watery Adonais
longs for thee—& Shelley three,
that's three—burn in salt
with slow most change—
We've had no crack at eternity
in a billion years of trying—

one grain of sand possesses
3 thousand worlds of glee—
not to mention me—
Ah sea

Ah si—Ah so—
shoot—shiver—mix—
ha roll—tara—ta ta—
curlurck—Kayash—Kee—
Pearls pearls in the yellow West
—Yellow sky to China—
Pacific we named here
water as always meeting
water—Pacific Pacific
Pacific tapfic—geroom—
gedowsh—gaka—gaya—

Tatha—gata—mana—
What sails used old bhikkus?
Dhikkus? Dhikkus!
What raft mailed Mose
to the hoven dovepost?
What saved Blackswirl

from the Kidd plank?
What Go-Bug here?
Seet! Seeeeeeeeeee
eeeeeee—kara—
Pounders out yar—

Big Sur they call this sand
these rocks this creek?
Raton Canyon by name pours
Coyote leaves & old Pomo bones
& old dust of Tomahawks
into your angler'd maw—
My salt maw shall salvage
Taylors—sewing in the room
below—
Sewing weed shrat for hikers
in the milky silt—
Sewing crosswards
for certainty—Sartan
are we of Price Victory
in this salt War with thee
& thine thee jellied yink!
Look O the sea here called
Pacific Sea!

Taki!

My golden empty soul'll
outlast yr salty sill
—the Windows of my jelly eye
& fish head muck look out on thee,
slit, with cigar-a-mouth,
some contempt—
Yet I hie me to see you
—you hie thee to eat
me—Fair in sight
and worn, aright—
Arra! Aroo!
Ger der va—

Silly silent cities in the sea
have children playing cardboard

mush with eignyard old Englander
beeplates slickered oer with scum
of histories below—
No tempest as still & awful
as the tempest within—
Sorcerer hip! Buddhalands
& Buddhaseas!
What sails Maudgalyayana used
he only knows to tell
but got kilt by yellers
sreaming down the cliff
"Let's go home!
Now!"
—leave marge smashed djamas

Maudgalyayana was murdered by the sea—
But the sea dont tell—
The sea dont murder—
The seadrang scholars
oughter know that
or
go back to School

Hear over there the ocean motor?
Feel the splawrsh of it?
Six silly centepedes here, Machree—
Ah Ratatatatatat—
the machinegun sea, rhythmic
balls of you pouring in
with smooth eglantinee
in yr pedigreed milkpup
tenor—
Tinder marsh aright arrooo—
arrac'h—arrache—
Kamac'h—monarc'h—
Kerarc'h Jevac'h—

Tamana—gavow—
Va—Voovla—Via—
Mia—mine—
sea
poo

Farewell, Sur—

Didja ever tell him
about water meeting water—?
O go back to otter—
Term—Term—Klerm
Kerm—Kurn—Cow—Kow—
Cash—Cac'h—Cluck—

Clock—Gomeat sea need
be deep I see you
Enoc'h
soon anarf
in Old Brittany

21 August 1960
Pacific Ocean at Big Sur
JACK KERAOUAC

Character Key

Jack Kerouac primarily wrote autobiographical stories based on his actual experiences. The following Character Key utilizes Kerouac's other novels, letters, and interviews to list the likely real-life models for the characters in *Big Sur*.

Character name	Actual person
Jack Duluoz	Jack Kerouac
Cody Pomeray	Neal Cassady
Evelyn	Carolyn Cassady
Lorenzo Monsanto	Lawrence Ferlinghetti
Irwin Garden	Allen Ginsberg
Româna Swartz	Lenore Kandel
Robert Browning	Robert LaVigne
Pat McLear	Michael McClure
Willamine "Billie" Dabney	Jackie Gibson Mercer
George Baso	Albert Saijo
Jarry Wagner	Gary Snyder
Arthur Wayne	Alan Watts
Dave Wain	Lew Welch
Ben Fagan	Philip Whalen
Arthur Ma	Victor Wong
Julien	Lucien Carr

Biographical Timeline

1922 Born Jean Louis Lebris de Kerouac in Lowell, Massachusetts, on March 12, the third child of Gabrielle and Leo Keroauc, French-Canadian immigrants to New England.

1926 Kerouac's brother, Gerard, dies of rheumatic fever at age 9.

1939 Graduates from Lowell High School with a scholarship to Columbia University.

1939 To fulfill scholarship requirement, attends Horace Mann Preparatory School in New York City for one year.

1940 Enrolls in Columbia College in New York City.

1941 Drops out after breaking his leg in a freshman football game.

1942 Sails to Greenland as merchant marine on S.S. Dorchester.

1943 Enlists in U.S. Navy, discharged on psychiatric grounds. Sails to Liverpool as merchant marine on S.S. George Weems. On his return, meets Edie Parker and Lucien Carr.

1944 Childhood friend Sebastien Sampas dies while serving in World War II. Through Carr, meets William S. Burroughs and Allen Ginsberg. Jailed as accessory and material witness in murder of David Kammerer who was killed by Lucien Carr. Bailed out by parents of girlfriend Edie Parker on condition that the two marry before he is released from jail.

1945 Begins writing *The Town and the City*. Collaborates with Burroughs on an unpublished novel, *And the Hippos Were Boiled in Their Tanks,* an account of the events surrounding the Kammerer murder.

1946 Kerouac's father, Leo, dies of cancer. Meets Neal Cassady.

Marriage with Edie Parker is annulled.

1947   Travels to Denver, California, and back to New York.

1948   Begins working on earliest version of *On the Road*.

1949   Travels with Cassady to Louisiana and San Francisco. Moves briefly to Colorado with mother. Visits San Francisco. Returns with Cassady to New York.

1950   *The Town and The City* (New York: Harcourt, Brace) is published. Moves to Denver.

1951   Drives with Cassady to Mexico. Returns to New York and marries Joan Haverty after a two-week courtship. Writes *On The Road*, a mostly autobiographical work of fiction that describes his road trip adventures across the United States and into Mexico with Cassady, the model for Dean Moriarty in the book, on a single roll of paper in three weeks. Separates from Joan Haverty. Moves to Neal Cassady's home in San Francisco to continue work on the novel.

1952   Writes *Doctor Sax* in Burroughs' apartment in Mexico City. Travels to North Carolina to visit sister Caroline in Rocky Mount, back to California where he works as a student brakeman and writes "The Railroad Earth," and Mexico before returning to New York. Daughter Jan Kerouac born in Albany, New York.

1953   Writes *Maggie Cassidy* while in New York. Travels to California to work for the railroad in San Jose. Takes job on S. S. William Carruth but goes AWOL in New Orleans and travels to New York. Writes *The Subterraneans*, a book about the brief affair he has there with Alene Lee.

1954   Visits Cassadys in San Jose. Studies Buddhism in New York and California. Called to court for failing to pay child support to Joan Haverty.

1955   Travels to Mexico City where he writes *Mexico City Blues* and begins *Tristessa*. Meets Gary Snyder and attends "Six Poets at the Six Gallery" reading in San Francisco where Ginsberg first reads "Howl."

1956   Writes *Visions of Gerard* in North Carolina. Travels to California and stays in Marin County. Writes *The Scripture of the Golden Eternity* and "Old Angel Midnight." Works as fire lookout in Mt. Baker-Snoqualmie National Forest, Washington, where he writes the journals that would become Book One of *Desolation Angels*. Finishes *Tristessa* in Mexico City. Returns to New York. Ginsberg's *Howl and Other Poems* published by City Lights in San Francisco.

1957   Travels to Tangier, Morocco, where he types and edits Burroughs' *Naked Lunch* with Ginsberg, then goes to Paris and London. After returning to New York he meets and lives with Joyce Johnson. Moves to Berkeley, California, with his mother. Visits Mexico City before moving to Orlando, Florida, with mother. Travels to New York. *On the Road* (New York: Viking Press) is published and Keroauc gives readings at the Village Vanguard. Writes *The Dharma Bums* in Orlando.

1958   Buys home in Northport, Long Island. *The Subterraneans* (New York: Grove Press) and *The Dharma Bums* (New York: Viking Press) are published. Neal Cassady sentenced to five years in San Quentin for possession of marijuana. Begins writing sketches for *Lonesome Traveler*.

1959   Narrates film *Pull My Daisy* in New York. Begins writing column for *Escapade*. A book of poetry, *Mexico City Blues* (New York: Grove Press), *Doctor Sax* (New York: Grove Press), and *Maggie Cassidy* (New York: Avon) are published. Travels to Los Angeles for Steve Allen Show appearance.

1960   Travels to California, stays at Bixby Canyon in Big Sur. Suffers alcohol withdrawal and nervous breakdown. A collection of short stories, *Lonesome Traveler* (New York: McGraw-Hill Book Co.), *Tristessa* (New York: Avon), and *Eternity* (Totem Press) are published.

1961   Moves to Orlando with mother. Travels to Mexico City, where
       he writes Book Two ("Passing Through") of *Desolation Angels*.
       Returns to Florida, where he writes *Big Sur*. *Book of Dreams*
       (San Francisco: City Lights) is published.

1962   Travels all over East Coast. *Big Sur* (New York: Farrar, Strauss,
       and Cudahy) is published.

1963   *Visions of Gerard* (New York Farrar, Strauss) is published.

1964   Sees Neal Cassady and attends Merry Pranksters party in New
       York. Sister Caroline dies.

1965   Travels to France. Writes *Satori In Paris*. *Desolation Angels*
       (New York: Coward-McCann) is published.

1966   *Satori In Paris* (New York: Grove) is published. Moves to
       Hyannis, on Cape Cod, with mother who then suffers a stroke.
       Marries Stella Sampas, sister of childhood friend Sebastian
       Sampas.

1967   Moves to Lowell with mother and Stella. Writes *Vanity of
       Duluoz*.

1968   Neal Cassady dies in Mexico. *Vanity of Duluoz* (New York:
       Coward-McCann) is published. Travels to Europe with Stella's
       brothers. Appears on Firing Line hosted by William F. Buckley.
       Moves with mother and Stella to St. Petersburg.

1969   Dies in St. Petersburg, Florida, on October 21 of abdominal
       hemorrhage due to complications associated with alcohol abuse.

Made in the USA
Middletown, DE
22 August 2024

59573920R00113